The
TALE
of the
TREES

a novella by

Cathie
Norton

SPECKLED PUPPY
PUBLISHING

Cover Design and Interior Formatting by Public Author
Cover Photo copyright © Toma Bonciu | Dreamstime.com
Interior Artwork copyright © Oleg Gur | Dreamstime.com
Author Photo by Manlouie Miller Design

Published by

Speckled Puppy
PUBLISHING

Dedication

*This book is dedicated
to all those who have lost
loved ones*

Acknowledgments

I'd like to thank the Writers' Gallery of Yucaipa, for without their expertise this book would not have been written.

Thanks to my husband Newell, for his undying support, and my sister Carol, for introducing us to our peaceful mountain retreat

Finally, thanks to Judith Ring, my editor, and to Eric Lorenzen, my coordinator and formatter. Also, thanks to Manlouie Miller Design for the wonderful author photos.

CHAPTER ONE

Katie sat at the table in their motorhome, exhausted and all cried out. She hadn't been able to stay home; the emptiness was too great, so she fled to Silent Glen, their mobile sanctuary, where they all shared consistent joy and relaxation, a cocoon of peace. Six months had passed since the death of her husband and daughter in that fiery crash in the Cajon Pass that left six dead and fifteen injured. A big rig jackknifed after it lost its brakes in the fog and crushed the car that carried Daniel and Casey. They died instantly but others were not as lucky. A family of four burned to death.

The enormous emptiness she felt engulfed her like a boat lost and adrift in a storm. It was as if an invisible shaft had been driven through her heart and now only loneliness existed. "There is no evidence of the hollowness I feel inside. My life, the one I once knew and loved, has been shattered, and only an empty shell is left. How can I ever go on or be whole again," she thought.

The raspberry vodka she sipped all evening dulled her senses. "I only hope it will help me sleep." She listened to the sound of the trees as the wind blew through their branches. It had always reminded her of the sound of ocean waves, rhythmic and soothing, but not now.

Katie got little sleep and when she did, she had recurrent nightmares about the families that burned to death and bloody bodies in the road. "Your family died upon impact. They never knew what hit them." The calm reassurance of the officer echoed in her mind but they were still gone.

The horror of the accident continued to haunt Katie, overwhelming her; her family was gone. "I feel guilty for not being with them that fateful day. I had to work. Damn you Daniel, why did you leave me like this?" she screamed into the emptiness of her life.

The crushing emotion of anger sat heavy on her heart. Devastation and constant sorrow enveloped her. It seemed impossible to get past that point of sadness. "All I can do is breathe, in and out, in and out, and just exist," She thought. How could she find hope in the immensity of her despair? She managed to work through the burial expenses, the funeral, the insurance claims, and the notifications and mounds of paper work. Alone she cursed and threw things as a release of her anger. "It feels good to let go of some of this tension," she told her parents. That is until she had to clean up the mess.

"I feel such an enormous void without Dan and Casey.

"I can't even think of going back to work now; my emotions are too raw. I can't face my own pain, much less that of my patients, families and friends. Patients in intensive care often teeter between life and death because of the extent of their injuries or illnesses. I'd be a basket case and need to be taken care of instead of caring for them."

Her parents had to help her through the first three weeks. They had put their lives on hold, but soon needed to return to Washington. Other friends and family assisted as time passed. "When everyone leaves is when I will feel the greatest burden of loss. I'll be alone and lonely when no one is here to distract me- no one for me to love."

Her mother called weekly, but Katie found it hard to explain what she felt, and so spent most of their conversation in tears and unable to carry on much of a conversation.

According to a friend and grief counselor, it could take up to two years to work through the shock of her loss. "Katie you can expect to experience five stages of grief; denial, anger, bargaining, depression, and acceptance or resolution" she said. "Some stages will take longer and they will flip-flop, following no order, rhyme or reason."

Denial would not be part of the equation, only the stark reality that her family would never again come home or be part of her life. When she was unable to sleep, she prayed it was just a bad dream, but they were both gone.

Katie continued to be angry, very angry, impaled with grief, and depressed most of the time. She blamed God and asked, "Why did you let it happen? How will I go on or ever feel whole again?"

Julianne, Katie's friend from high school and fellow nurse at the hospital, offered heart-felt support. She also kept Katie informed on the latest at the work. "I don't really care and can't concentrate on my career now," she told her. Their friendship went deep and Julianne continued to be a great source of support as the days and weeks passed.

With the devastating news of the accident that August day, Julianne had supported her and drove her home from work. Katie sat, tears streaming down her face, in a daze. Julianne called and visited Katie on a routine basis but really didn't know how best to help. She just listened and held Katie when she needed someone to lean on.

"Simply being able to talk about my feelings comforts me. It soothes a tiny bit of the unrelenting pain and loss. It also feels good to have someone listen to me, without judgment, and it gives me solace in many ways," she told Julianne through her tears. "I hate it when people say God needed them or the pain will lessen with time. I know they mean well but they have no idea how little it helps and how much it hurts. In fact I'd rather they say nothing at all."

Katie continued to sip the vodka. Alcohol had never been a vice. She enjoyed a glass of fine wine or a cocktail when they dined out but never made a habit of it. She had discovered raspberry vodka in a martini when she and Dan took a cruise out of New Orleans. Now the liquor dulled the fact that her loved ones were gone forever. Her reliance on it would have to stop, but not yet, for it numbed the pain.

After the funeral, her family returned to their own lives. She now was totally alone and overwhelmed with emptiness. She couldn't face the devastation and loneliness of their home as the memory of Dan and Casey's death felt like a rock in the pit of her stomach. Now when she passed Casey's room or entered their bedroom, it hurt too much. No parent should ever outlive their child. It was unnatural and beyond comprehension.

Casey's bed had been hastily made the day of the accident, and it showed in the uneven comforter and numerous wrinkles. Her shoes and socks were scattered around the room, as were her many favorite stuffed animals. She closed her daughter's door-she couldn't bear the thought of her child never growing up.

Casey had just turned five the previous January. Katie would never experience the joy of sending her off to her first day of kindergarten. Never be a room mother, a Brownie leader, attend dance recitals, nor ever enjoy her daughter's first date, watch love bloom, attend her graduation from high school or be the mother of the bride, never, never, never.

The thought brought to mind the young patient, Larry, she and Julianne had cared for earlier that fateful day, the boy with obvious head injury. He had catapulted over the handle bars of his quad, head first into a large rock. He had been showing off for his friends and hadn't worn a helmet. Surgery revealed the extent of his massive head injury. Larry was brain dead. His mother apparently arrived on the scene prior to the paramedics and found Larry unconscious. He would never regain consciousness. Katie sat at the bedside and held his hand as the doctor turned off the ventilator and remove the breathing tube. His heart stopped and Larry was pronounced dead.

Katie had held Larry's mother in her arms as she sobbed. Katie now knew the complete devastation Larry's mother had felt the emptiness, and the absolute desolation of the poor woman's loss.

CHAPTER TWO

Katie awoke suddenly with a start by just a hint of a whisper, a song, a lullaby. A lullaby, definitely, by the singsong breathy words and music, but it was an unfamiliar language, maybe Native American. She glanced out of the coach window and noticed the movement of the branches of the trees, but nothing that would account for what sounded like a song. Katie shook her head and tried to remember where she was. It took her a few seconds to remember that she was in her motor home in Silent Glen, her home away from home.

Dan had acted like a puppy with a new bone when it came to driving their motorhome, and she had not yet taken the opportunity to learn to drive it. For now it was stored in the mountain retreat. The staff would place it in a designated site when she called them. Someday she would master the act of learning to drive it. "Maybe I'll tour all the other places we dreamed of seeing? We were able to tour the coast of California, Oregon and Washington and enjoy the spectacular beaches when Casey was just a baby." Great memories she thought and then the realization hit that she sat in their motor home without her family.

Her head felt fuzzy from the vodka and she thought it possible she had dreamed the lullaby. Maybe it had been the rustling of leaves and the haunting wind through the trees. Her dreams, when she did sleep, were always strange, and full of fear and helplessness. No, the singing continued and she knew she was awake.

She opened the door slowly. The soft music kept going, but now distant drums and a flute accompanied the singing. The moon appeared as just a silver sliver in an ebony sky with pinhole dots of stars. The heavens always made her feel small and insignificant, but now they offered a sense of oneness with the universe and her loved ones, something she hadn't felt in the last six months. She breathed in the fresh air, said a silent prayer, "God help me through the night to let go and find peace." She then closed the door and returned to the sofa hoping she could sleep.

As morning dawned Katie dressed and started to walk aimlessly around the huge campsite. She ambled through the almost deserted campground, not really seeing, simply existing. She found relief in moving instead of sitting, ruminating on what she would never again be, a family. She was now a widow; a fact she constantly found hard to get her mind around. What would give her purpose in life now that her family was gone?

Katie continued to walk in a dream-like state as a light fog settled into the valley. She found herself in the most rural part of the camp. The trees were nestled closer together among the numerous boulders in the area, rocks stacked and much flatter than those in other sections of the park. Some had hollowed-out areas in them. A rustic wooded bridle path led into the forested area and she climbed on a low fallen tree trunk next to the bridge. Beautiful, but rugged, because it overlooked what could be a stream. Tears fell without warning. When she finally regained her composure, out of the corner of her eye, she caught a slight movement and felt a distinctive presence. Just beyond the tree line a women stood in the shadows.

Unaware of the passage of time, and in her present state of mind, she felt, or imagined an Indian girl, with long black braided hair interwoven with feathers. Katie watched as the girl crushed what looked like seeds into a fine powder in the indentations of the rock. She sat fascinated by the girl's movements watching the image projected in the fog. As she studied the girl in the hazy light, others appeared to join her; in fact entire families, and then a village appeared. They all had brown skin, wore long black braids, and were clothed in animal skins. I must be dreaming, Katie thought.

Katie watched in amazement as the people moved around the village as if she didn't exist. Huts dotted the background constructed of some sort of bark and hides from animals. Maybe she was the apparition. During the brief encounter, she experienced an overwhelming sense of belonging and she again blinked back tears, but tears of joy. Then as suddenly as the vision had materialized, it vanished. Katie shook her head and wondered if she had fallen asleep. What just happened?

Time was the enemy. She had nothing to look forward to, or anyone to wait for, only the heavy loneliness. This was even more apparent after she watched the families.

Katie's teeth chattered and she started to shiver so she rose, stiff after sitting in the cold for God knew how long. Then she slowly made her way back to her RV as it began to drizzle. She now, more acutely aware of her surroundings, began to ponder the age of the area, the landscape, but most of all the ancient trees. She arrived and entered the coach, still shivering and now bone-tired. She poured herself a cup of day-old coffee then heated it in the microwave.

Cathie Norton

CHAPTER THREE

Memories flooded her mind whenever she entered her home. Katie couldn't escape up the mountain all the time. She sat cross-legged on the floor in the living room, her picture album in her lap and tenderly touched each picture. The infamous blue and white Chevy convertible stared back at her. Dan stood shirtless, proud, with a shit-eating grin on his face. His friend Russell stood next to him. They had double-dated in that car. Katie fondly remembered riding in it with the top down. She always felt a sense of freedom with her hair whipping around her face. They sat under the stars at the drive-in movies and drank frosty A & W root beer in mugs almost too cold to hold.

She and Casey had heard many stories about Dan's regrets that he had to sell his car before he went into the Navy. Doug, his so-called friend, promised to keep it up and when Dan returned, sell it back to him. At his discharge from the military, Dan found the car already sold and impossible to trace to its whereabouts. His consistent goal since then was to repurchase it or one similar.

Dan had called about a 55 Chevy advertised in Victorville and arranged to go see it. If the price seemed right, his ideal car would be his and the memories again tangible. One could feel the palpable excitement in the air that fateful morning when Dan and Casey left the house.

"They would still be alive if it wasn't for that damn car" Katie screamed, as if scolding Dan.

Katie stood in front of the mirror to brush her hair and

reached into the drawer and came up with Casey's hair ribbons. Memories of the birth of the child they tried for so long to conceive flooded her mind. Casey arrived with great fanfare. The suitcase stood packed and ready, waiting at the door for a month until the right moment arrived. Dan, his mother and Katie's mother crowded the labor room as Cassandra Lynn arrived; each thrilled to hear her first cry. Labor had been easy, if you could call it that, lasting only five hours. The contractions started about ten thirty in the evening and Casey made her grand entrance at two- fifteen in the morning.

One had to be a mother to feel the immense ecstasy, the impact of motherhood, and the sense of completeness giving birth. Everyone in the room shouted of joy. Casey resembled an angel, perfect from the first moment. No misshapen head or ruddy completion from the delivery. A contented baby, even though she remained extremely active when awake, just like before she was born. What a privilege to be the mother of such a jubilant child. Now her child, her angel, had returned to heaven.

As she examined the photographs, her wistfulness continued. Memories flooded her mind of Dan's proposal that crisp September day, under the gigantic oak tree at the college. She was in nursing school and one Sunday after church they took a drive in his Chevy, top down, even though the weather was chilly. She had packed a picnic lunch and the empty campus offered an ideal place to enjoy it. After lunch they walked the area then returned to the tree where Dan got down on one knee and asked for her hand in marriage. "It was the happiest moment of my life that is until our wedding day. Then Casey's birth topped any other joy I could imagine. What great memories I have," Katie told the albums as if they would respond.

Before the birth of their daughter, Katie and Dan took a cruise that left and returned to New Orleans. They arrived a day early to explore before they headed to the Caribbean. "I vividly remember we sat by the crackling fire in the downstairs lounge listening to a three- piece jazz combo. That's where I experienced the cosmopolitan with raspberry vodka." I wanted something different and the waitress suggested the Cosmopolitan martini.

"An elegant drink for an elegant lady," Dan said.

"We wandered the streets on that chilly night with Dan's arm around me and looked in the windows at all of the antique stores. We arrived a few weeks before Mardi Gras and some of the street vendors threw the colorful gold, green and bright pink beads." Katie spoke as if she was telling the story to someone for the first time and sighed at the wonderful memories.

"We were treated royally on the seven-day cruise with its crystal blue waters, flying fish, relaxing strolls on the deck, excursions to tropical islands, gourmet meals, and many playful times. I was fascinated by scuba diving and blown away by the fish that came up to your goggles as if your eyes were fish food. Schools of colorful neon yellow, blues, greens and red fish swam undisturbed by humans. Some had multi-colors, stripes, and others were plaid. I'd never seen such beauty before. The ship returned to port all too soon but we knew we had another adventure awaiting us.

"In New Orleans we wandered around the town, enthralled with the wonder of all the new sights, sounds, smells, varieties of food, and the amazing shops, and street vendors. We ate poor boy and muffuletta sandwiches, seafood creole, and jambalaya and frequently enjoyed oysters and watched in fascination as they were shucked. It took a talent and skilled hand to shuck an oyster. The beignets and chicory coffee were staples each morning before we started a new day of exploration. We enjoyed three more days of adventure before we headed home to California."

"The tour of the above-ground cemeteries continued our adventure with the ornate carvings and multiple family names. The guide explained all graves were above ground because of the high water table. It seemed creepy that multiple generations baked in the sun and turned to dust. After the right amount of time the chutes between the top and bottom of the grave was pulled and they were all entombed together. The trees around the graves were strange as well but native to the area. They swayed and the leaves rustled making an eerie sound. Dan and I were intrigued by the interesting people, their folk-lore, stories of ghosts, practices of black magic, and history of voodoo."

"We strolled down the brick walk of Bourbon Street holding hands, and a woman in a brightly-lit shop with colorful hanging boas in all colors of the rainbow, asked if they were newlyweds.

"Is it only newlyweds that hold hands?" Dan whispered to me.

We both laughed. It only shows that romance and love are timeless. Timeless, Katie thought and continued her conversation with the album and surrounding furniture.

"The cruise to the Caribbean and the exciting, yet lazy outing in New Orleans is as if we had experienced two entirely different vacations, all in one," they told their friends. As she reminisced, gesturing to the air about all of the great times, reality hit her like a slap in the face. They would never again share anything. She closed the album and sat and stared into space. "God, why did this happen to us?"

CHAPTER FOUR

Her thoughts drifted back to their established habits. Going to bed would not be the same without the familiar pat on the butt, a ritual established since the first day they were married, ten years before. Katie now often slept, if you could call it that, on the sofa or in Dan's recliner. She'd never like sitting in his recliner before, but it brought her closer to him. It had been his favorite place besides the garage. He'd often teased and told her "it was the only real space of his in their home."

Dan frequently voiced the same thing about their motor home. When they camped, her responsibility was to take care of the inside, and his, the outside, but the RV really belonged to him.

Others encouraged her to go through his clothes and give them away so she could "move on with her life." She didn't really want to move on, and when she did go home, every time she opened his closet, she found herself weeping uncontrollably. She even found his favorite denim shirt, the one with his familiar masculine scent and a hint of Paul Saladin cologne. He'd left it hanging on the bedpost. She now wore it most of the time just to be a little closer to him. She didn't wash it for fear the familiar fragrance would be lost forever. It was the only part of him she had left.

Dan had collected baseball caps on vacations or when he visited new places. What was she supposed to do with those? More than a hundred hung in rows above the windows and doors in the computer room. She avoided that room as well since she basically closed up the house. One day she would start with things not as personal, and gradually "liberate" them. She would make sure they went to someone who either wanted them for their own memories, or needed them. She still couldn't bring herself to think about looking through Dan's and Casey's closets. Going through their things hurt too much. Casey's room remained especially daunting.

The photographs brought back rich memories. Tears slipped from her eyes and warmly bathed her cheeks. Her mind drifted back, as she fondly remembered their first date. Katie vividly recalled the time she spent it took to select her clothing and dress for the evening. "I want to be perfect for our date" she had told her mother. Their first kiss and the tenderness gave her the sensation of floating. All of his kisses did and it never ceased to amaze me. The warmth of his lips, the way their hearts beat as one with every hug. Dan wasn't shy about expressing his love and the strong feelings he had, since the first time he saw her as she walked home from school. "I loved that green and white striped sweater. It looked really great on you," he had told her. "These memories I will always treasure, forever."

Times, many times, the impact and passion of their love amazed her as it grew deeper and more intense with each year. The richness, gravity of emotion, the shared oneness constantly flabbergasted her as they increased throughout their years of marriage. Now she would never experience that wonderful heartwarming feeling again.

The specialness of their love continued when Dan booked the Hotel Del Coronado for their tenth anniversary, the month before the accident. Each day they took long walks on the beach and played in the sand. They dined at the finest restaurants, made love on the beach in the moon-light, drank champagne, and then ate strawberries and chocolate in bed. They slept late and took the opportunity for lazy afternoon naps which had been impossible with an active five-year-old whirlwind at home. Casey's energy never ran short and the only time she wasn't active was when peacefully asleep.

Katie had made arrangements for Casey to stay with her

parents so she and Dan could have time away, the first time since her daughter's birth. In hindsight, the time with him would be treasured forever. Casey's grandparents planned a trip to Disneyland. They stayed in a hotel for two days, a first for Casey, and basked in the wonders of Disneyland and California adventure. She and Dan relished the time alone, but called routinely to check in with her parents. She got her daughter on the phone and Casey breathlessly chattered nonstop relating tales of princesses, Mickey Mouse and stories of wonderful sights, rides and of course, the castle. She and Dan laughed so hard they almost wet their pants.

The loneliness and memory stirred by the pictures of her family, now gone, became too painful to tolerate, she closed the album. She could no longer stay at home. She returned the albums in their place of honor, locked the house and returned to her mountain retreat and the cocoon of their motor home. She arrived in the dark and retreated to the recliner where she again dozed off into a fitful sleep as her memories were clouded.

Cathie Norton

CHAPTER FIVE

The pouring rain pounded on the coach's roof and an electric charge in the air was palpable. Katie always delighted in the rain and its results. It cleaned the air and made everything reinvigorated and pristine. It washed away all the dirt and grime and left behind an exhilarating and refreshing fragrance. The reassuring sound lulled Katie into a deep, peaceful sleep, and as she drifted off, the shower bathed and soothed her aching heart. She awakened refreshed from the first full night sleep she'd experienced in days to the sounded of a pan flute. As she awoke in the recliner, the sun shone directly into her eyes, through the window above the sofa where she'd been sleeping since losing her family.

When she looked out the window, she discovered that the sound she heard was comprised of the gentle wind that whispered through a multitude of magnificent oak trees. Her head felt as though cobwebs encircled her brain, and because of the depth of her sleep, it took her a while to totally awaken. She hadn't yet slept in either of the beds she and Dan had shared. She couldn't face that reality yet.

The family enjoyed their home away from home in the mountain paradise. Her family frequently took round-trip tours on the facility bus when a sleepy-headed child was too tired to walk back from the pool. The driver relished offering obscure facts and a brief history of the area. It included specific information about the Ivah Indians. They were the original inhabitants of the area before the Temecula Indians, who resided in the valley below, raided the peaceful tribe. Apparently, according to the guide, it wiped out their entire population.

The bus driver told of a drought that had caused severe famine and scarcity of water. A rival tribe came upon the peaceful natives as they gathered chia grain, a food staple, and overwhelmed them. They attacked the Ivah as they sat on the plateau by the semi-circular precipice. The braves and their families had no time to collect weapons to defend themselves. Every man, woman and child were either killed outright or pushed over the edge of the cliff. All men, women and children were killed, or were they?

The informational account of the native people added to the ambiance of the campground. Casey had always enjoyed stories and the one about the area intrigued their little girl the most, with Indians living in the area, "real Indians," she always stated, emphasized that made her eyes shine an even brighter blue. "I have never met real Indians." Casey would always say. The driver would make a point of telling more stories every time they rode the bus.

Casey liked the large flat rocks with multiple hollows embedded in them, mutates, that were scattered around the upper camping area. She liked to imagine grinding grain into flour. "Mommy, that's how they made bread and fed their people." she would say.

Casey pointed to the rocks, "They could have used them for tables." Long past were the tribal communities; the residents were long gone. The history was sketchy at best for only a few facts were known and no written records existed. The Indian story-tellers told only of conquest, but not the circumstances of the extinct Indian tribe.

She and Dan had purchased the membership at Silent Glen in Poppet Flats six years earlier. The campground resided in the towering majesty of Mount San Jacinto (Saint-Hyacinth). It stood over ten thousand feet at its peak, up the hill from the Banning and Beaumont area. Her sister Carol and her husband had discovered the secluded, peaceful campsite.

"You need to join so we can camp together," she told Katie.

They never regretted joining the lovely place with all of its amenities. Only thirty minutes from their home, but three thousand miles away from reality and their busy lives.

The family had fun paddling around the pool on hot summer days and it invigorated everyone. The seniors were funny with their noodles, tubular floats, lazily propelling their bodies through the water. They felt no need to worry about their physique, their actions or swim wear. The fact that seniors gather girth as they aged did not seem to bother anyone. The peaceful days passed, often with game playing and pool frolic, the excitement of the day.

Even though Casey was only five years old, she had mastered the game of rummy cubes, frequently winning with glee. When the weather became too hot, game playing and visits to the pool took up the entire day. A chocolate and vanilla swirl ice cream cone completed the adventure. The area provided a wealth of opportunities for young people from crafts to miniature golf, extremely thrilling for someone Casey's age. With all of the excitement and fun, her daughter occasionally needed a nap. This gave her parents a chance to speak in adult terms. With children it is always a peanut-butter-and-jelly conversation and most often related to them. Katie and Dan relish their adult time.

They enjoyed long walks as Casey often rode her pink bike with training wheels and a bell, calling out "beep, beep" when they passed others strolling through the park. Even though petite, she possessed a strong and athletic body. Everyone they encountered smiled with knowing looks, probably reliving their own family memories. Casey, a towheaded blond, had long curly locks, often in a French braid because of the fineness of her hair. It was easier to manage that way but there were the curls that always managed to escape on either side of her face and on top where it almost appeared as a halo. Often others would stop and comment on her angelic appearance. Now, Katie thought, she really is an angel.

Cathie Norton

CHAPTER SIX

Katie felt more at peace returning to her coach. It was too lonely at home and her heart continued to ache. In her RV she didn't have to think about going through their belongings. She often walked aimlessly around the area where the native people once lived. The dwellings no longer existed, but the trees and stones survived time.

As Katie sat near the flat stones she again heard the lullaby. She could see no one, but felt a tangible presence nevertheless. It provided a sense of tranquility and the same peace she sensed the first time she heard the soothing song. She decided at that very moment, to research the history of the mountain residents.

She returned to the coach and went directly to her computer to pull up information on the Indian tribes in the area before the white men settled. Katie searched the web until quite late and she grew tired and decided to continue the pursuit of the history in the morning. She had a purpose, a goal now, something she hadn't had since her family's death. She would discover the past and find out who the mysterious woman could be and why the lullaby?

The next morning she washed her face, brushed her teeth, and made one of the hardest decisions she would ever make, to resume her life without those she loved. There would be no familiar smell of fresh brewed coffee, or the sound Dan's morning cough. The memories would always be a part of her, but she needed to live even if they hadn't.

Casey would never run to her with hugs and butterfly kisses.

The hollow feeling still overwhelmed her, but Dan would want her to live, not just exist. If the tables were turned, she would want him to find peace and restart his life even though it would be different. She continued to ponder the situation as she dressed, unlocked the door and took her first step forward, alone now, without her family, but with a new purpose.

In the evening, the breeze and the rustle of leaves in the majestic oak trees felt as though they communicated with one another, maybe trying to convey their story to her. One could imagine the trees being interconnected even through time. From the moment of life as a tiny shoots and through hundreds of years, the trees had stood through rain, wind, and even fire. Scrubs, bushes and many types of trees also occupied the area but the grand oaks possessed and controlled the environment. If only the trees could share the tales of the area and its inhabitants. "What story would they tell? Would they divulge the history of the mountains or keep it secrets?" Katie said out loud as if attempting to convince the trees to give up their information. She talked to herself more frequently, having no one with which to share her thoughts. Katie sat and watched the movement of the grand guardians of the mountain and sensed the need to continue her exploration of the area.

CHAPTER SEVEN

With the grand oaks in mind, Katie's thoughts drifted back to the trees in her own back yard. Many a time she and Dan had sat on the patio watching Casey on her swing set. When the wind blew, it started at the west end of the community and progressed toward their home. The sound reminded her of a creek and its rushing water. It seemed like a strange phenomenon. The wind vibrated through the trees as if they were relating with one another before the breeze reached their still Elm. Then it dissipated into just a whisper. Katie wondered if the trees had a story to tell, if only humans could understand it. Maybe the trees in the campground were attempting to convey the tale of their area, the lullaby and the mystery woman by the bridge.

Her computer was now her companion and diversion from reality, as she continued the search for information. She discovered that the Montezuma tribes had settled the lower slopes of the San Jacinto Mountains and valleys around 1100 AD and were comprised of seven to ten tribal families. Most important on the list were the Ivah, Soboba, and Serrano Indians some familiar to the area today. Apparently many of the tribes took refuge in the mountain areas to escape the scorching heat of the barren desert below. At times the groups warred with one another, usually over food or water. The tribe in the pass and mountain areas resided in the area of Poppet Flats and Idyllwild.

What fascinates me is that the Native Americans of Poppet Flats cultivated sixty percent of the resources utilized for subsistence, Katie said out load as if telling someone else. The raw materials they harvested for food were ironwood, oak, ocotillo, manzanita, buckthorn, chai, and barrel cacti, something not even heard of today. Apparently the rich black soil known as "miken" nurtured the crops.

On further study she found they housed themselves in shelters that were made of bark from cedars and other trees, which provided a cool environment in the summer and warmth in the winter. She recalled seeing the huts in the vision while seated close to the bridge. Tribes that live in what is now Banning and Beaumont were different. Some known today are the Morongo, Temecula, and Aqua Caliente. Katie was aware of some of the Native American history because of the Indian names of places and cities that dot the valley and surrounding areas.

Further out from the mountain and nearby valleys lived other tribes, such as the Mojave Indians. In the summer those tribes occasionally took residence in the hills, and on the slopes of Mt. Jacinto. Because no written language had been established, all history was passed down from generation to generation by way of storytelling. Eventually many stories were lost as the tribes disbanded, were killed, or were blended into other groups.

Katie found herself working late into the night fascinated by the rich history of the area. As she explored further, she discovered the accounts and migration were documented only when white men came west.

White men moved west and took the Indians land that they had occupied for thousands of years. Keeping the tribal names straight became difficult because there were so many of them in the area. The white man often gave the local individuals familiar names from their own culture. Many towns, streets and local areas maintained the Native American names however. How could she accurately trace those who inhabited the lovely area of the mountains above Banning and Beaumont? What had happened to them?

According to her research, many rock carvings and pictographs of hunting scenes in vivid colors had been discovered in the surrounding hillsides and area of Silent Glen and Idyllwild. "I'll investigate them later, but I'm truly exhausted from my long hours of research. I need to sleep."

Cathie Norton

CHAPTER EIGHT

With a start Katie awoke in the dusk, and felt someone watching her. When she scanned the area through the window, she saw no one, but the same haunting lullaby enfolded her and a light breeze blew. She stepped outside her motorhome and noticed the shadow of a young Indian maiden. She walked slowly toward the girl and when Katie spoke, the image disappeared.

Katie sat on a nearby picnic bench a short distance from the coach and let her thoughts rise like smoke into the air. Eventually the stars materialized in the black sky and stood out like diamonds in vibrant hues of white, yellow, and blue. Though deserted, the atmosphere possessed the same sense of peace she felt the first time she heard the lullaby.

Residents reported that the ghosts of the mountain ancestors continued to inhabit the area. The stories told were that they would not let go of their land. Katie wondered if the young girl haunted the area, or if her imagination played tricks on her, especially because of the loss of her daughter.

Katie walked slowly back into the motorhome and discovered that she was surprisingly hungry, something she hadn't really felt since before her family's death. She made herself a tuna sandwich, ate an entire bag of Cheetos, and then poured herself a tall glass of milk. It tasted really good for some reason. She no longer drank vodka to escape reality. Instead the intrigue of her surroundings and the people who once populated the area tempered her need to escape. She returned to her research.

Whenever Katie felt the acute loss creeping into her soul, she went to the computer and focused her energy on the history of the mountain. This act prevented her from concentrating on her loneliness.

As she further investigated the history of the area, and its people, she found information about John Muir. As he surveyed the area, he found rock carvings and pictograms. According to what she read, the pictographs had yet to be deciphered. Symbols like sun wheels, led the researchers to speculate on the possibility an earlier oriental occupation in the area. Rocks had been found in Fern Valley, a distance away, were known to have pictographs in bright red of hunting scenes.

As Katie traveled up the mountain from her home in the valley she noticed a hollowed out area of red rock on the left side of the steep mountain. Due to her studies and now acutely aware of things she had never really noticed before. She stopped her car to better examine the unnatural crevasse, and noticed the rocks seemed unusually formed. She could see markings in the hollow but from her vantage point they were too high to inspect. The area was half way up the tall ridge on the opposite side of the travel lane and impossible to investigate.

Katie continued her research, and found that famine and drought in the area caused tribal upheaval, competition for food, and fighting for optimal land and resources. The tale of the generally peaceful Ivah society, told of capture and slaughter by the Temecula tribe. The story of the inhabitants falling to death by being pushed off cliffs continued to surface; however no records of any kind could be found, especially of possible survivors. Were there people who avoided the disaster?

Day after day she reviewed multiple references to the area. A legend existed about the Tahquitz peak, of the gigantic finger-like rock that rose eight thousand feet into the air, jutted up into the sky as though reaching for the heavens. It lies on the east side of the village of Idyllwild. The story went that it was the home of the Nakat, a primal evil spirit that devoured the souls of those it captured. Today the area is known as Lily Rock, named by Stanford Eastman of the Southern California Colony Association. The once barren surrounding area is now named

Riverside. The tale goes that Stanford named the rock after his daughter. Another common rendition of its name is that it is white like a lily. Climbers today continue to call it Tahquitz rock.

An old folktale tells of a beautiful Indian princess, Mena, the daughter of the chief of the Sobobas. They occupied Poppet Flats along with the Ivahs at one point in time. Tahquitz braves kidnapped Mena but the princess's betrothed followed them and was able to free the princess. They reunited at what is now known as Lunch Rock, which lies at the base of Lily Rock. There they found a cave in which to hide and escape the approaching Tahquitz tribesmen, but an earthquake entombed the couple inside with a huge bolder covering the entrance. Since then, the area is said to be haunted. Sounds of someone scraping and dirt moving can be heard, especially during certain summer months.

Katie wondered if the vision of the lovely girl in the mist had something to do with the story of the couple. Perhaps they were attempting to return to their homeland, their people. The lullaby brought Katie peace. Maybe the comfort Katie felt, provided by the vision, could be transferred to assist those trapped inside the cave. If she could find a way she might be able to aid the princess and her intended to transcend to the great unknown. What joy she would feel by resolving Mena's traumatic death, as well as those she loved. A curse could be reversed couldn't it? She decided she would inquire about it and visit the rock that covered the cave's entrance. She wanted to see if she could connect with the apparition, and attempt to aid them to pass beyond this earthly realm.

Cathie Norton

CHAPTER NINE

"It's time to take the next step in my grief recovery. I will sleep in our motorhome bed, the one Dan and I shared. The one I haven't been able to face since his death." As Katie climbed into bed and rested her head on the pillow, she drifted into peaceful sleep. Dreams engulfed her slumber but were just beyond her grasp when she awoke. She did remember seeing a willowy woman in Indian garb. She had a long braid intertwined with feathers and amethyst-colored beads. Unfortunately, the woman's face was out of focus. Her dream provided a sense of tranquility, which replaced the dreams of the crash.

On one of her daily walks around the park, she stopped by the registration office and inquired about the history of the surrounding area. But the staff member knew only about the massacre on the mountain, something already known to Katie. She now found herself continually drawn into the mystery and intrigue of the area. She returned to her computer to ferret out any further information she could find.

As she let her mind wander, scanning the information collected, she could imagine the progressive occupation of the area. The 1800s brought many a pioneer to the area, such as Paulino Weaver from Mexico. He acquired Rancho San Gorgonio and lived among the Indians. Later the first white man, Dr. Isaac Smith, came and, eventually purchased the ranch and built a hotel and stage-coach stop. The space would provide a comfort station between Los Angles and the desert on long, uncomfortable stagecoach journeys. As her fantasy continued, she could picture Dr. Smith befriending the chief of the tribe, Juan Antonio, and the doctor aided the warriors in protecting the white man's settlement. It saddened her to realize that Juan later died of smallpox, one of the diseases brought by the white-man. Other diseases introduced to the native population were syphilis, diphtheria, chicken pox and measles and pneumonia which caused numerous deaths. The shaman medicine men had no remedies for the white-man's diseases. The Banning Pass area documented parts of the history but she could find nothing further on Silent Glen.

Katie drove down the hill and stopped at the market to restock her supplies. A woman approached her with a look of concern, asking if she needed help. The lady, visibly shaken, asked if Katie had been ill because of her appearance. Her skin was almost translucent and her face gaunt, while her clothes hung on her frame like the pictures of those from concentration camps. The woman had seen Katie almost faint at the meat counter and watched her sit on the counters edge to keep from falling. Katie started to sob uncontrollably and had to sit down before she did faint. Others surrounded her now and the manager of the store called the paramedics. She declined their advice to go to the hospital, but accepted a drink of cold water and a banana. When she gained control and felt a little stronger she finished her shopping.

Embarrassed at what had just happened made Katie realize she needed to pull herself together, eat, even if she wasn't hungry, and continue to find a way to go on, to begin a new life. She gathered the groceries to restock her home refrigerator and threw away all of the spoiled food. Her next task was to tackle the cupboards.

CHAPTER TEN

A knock on the door interrupted the flow of her task at hand. She glanced in the mirror on her way to answer it and became acutely aware of why the lady in the store had voiced such concern. Looking back at her was someone she didn't recognize. She saw only a shadow of her prior self. Her face was drawn, sallow in color and her cheeks hollow. Her eyes were sunken with no spark of life, where before they held an endless twinkle of excitement. Katie's hair, which had shown golden like her daughter's, now hung limp and lifeless. She considered herself an attractive woman, but it definitely wasn't apparent now.

The lady at the door was dark-skinned, with high cheek bones, and a bulky frame. She wore a loose tunic type dress in brown, with earth-tone beads around the neck and hem. Her skin appeared weathered; Katie guessed her age at around eighty. What seemed odd was that Katie had the feeling somehow she was familiar. The old woman watched Katie like a hawk and offered her a leather-bound book. She then turned and simply walked away.

Katie stood as if frozen, until the woman disappeared, then closed and locked the door. She opened the soft leather book and found the pages blank. She hurriedly opened the door again, determined to find the old woman to ask her the reason she gave her the book, but she was gone. Katie went to the living room, sat in Dan's recliner and stared out the bay window while she pondered the gift. Katie rested her head on the back of the chair and fell fast asleep. Numerous dreams drifted through her mind, but surprisingly when she awoke she felt rested.

She walked around the house, went to Casey's room and out of habit, tidied the room, rearranged the stuffed animals on the bed then opened the closet. There hung all of the lovely clothes her daughter had enjoyed. An array of colorful outfits in shades pink, Casey's favorite, filled the closet. The chest of dress-up clothes sat on the floor open, and a red sequined dress hung over the side. There, two boas, one bright pink and the other sunshine yellow, peeked out from the chest. Katie picked them up and lovingly folded each, then replaced everything neatly in the trunk. "Some little girl needs to enjoy these things."

It was time to start the long process of release. She would proceed slowly, tenderly remember her little girl and the pleasure she brought to their entire family. Katie would always treasure that joy.

Katie entered their bedroom, took a deep breath and opened Dan's closet door. His side of the closet was always a mess, with clothes on the floor and the shirts not buttoned as they hung slightly askew. Before, it had irritated her that he couldn't keep things tidy, but now it reminded her of all of his endearing qualities. The special person she had married.

She would start the process of letting go, difficult but necessary. Step-by-step Katie packed up half of Dan's things. I feel so empty and my heart hurts she told the room. Little-by-little she would progress through all of his things. Large boxes from the garage would house all of his clothes, shoes and other belongings. It was time to get on with her life and this would help.

Katie kept special articles of clothing, his favorite patriotic shirt with the flags on it, another shirt with fifty-sixty type cars, and some golf shirts, the comfortable ones he especially liked when he golfed with his buddies. Family members and friends could wear some of the shirts, but it would be difficult to find a person who could wear his pants. He was not very tall in stature, but was a giant of a man in love and affection. Strangely, she felt a sense of relief as she stroked and tenderly folded each piece of clothing and gently placed each in the box. She closed the closet door and with that very motion a feather like feeling, that of moving forward, lay gently on her heart.

She would take her time, and quit when it became overwhelming. The healing process would take time to complete, but she had conquered the initial course of action. "I need to take one step at a time," she said out loud just to reassure herself. Katie remembered her friend who told her about the five stages of grief and the importance of giving herself space as she vacillated between each step as she healed. She needed to be as kind to herself as she would be to others.

To her surprise her stomach growled and she felt hungry. She had ignored the hollowness in her gut because the void in her heart overwhelmed the other sensation since that terrible day. "I'll tackle the rest of the closet and the chest of drawers soon. It may take me a few days, weeks or months," she told the closet, with a half-smile. "I will find the strength to slowly continue and make progress with Dan's belongings; eventually I'll tackle Casey's room."

After satisfying her hunger it was time for bed. Tired, Katie entered the bathroom and prepared to put on her favorite PJs. She washed her face, brushed her hair and would brush her teeth. She opened the medicine cabinet and two tubes of paste fell out, she grabbed the nearest one and proceeded to open the cap to place the goo on her tooth brush. She examined the paste only to find it to be Ben Gay. A smile crossed her lips and then a chuckle escaped.

She vividly remembered the story her grandfather told of his brother Charlie. After a long night of partying, Charlie arose the next morning hung over with a pounding headache and a mouth that felt like the army had marched through it with dirty boots. He went to the bathroom to brush his teeth and relieve his hangover. He placed a large swirl of paste on the brush, the kind shown in a commercial. It filled the bristles with a swirl at the end. He then scrubbed vigorously. Great- Uncle Charlie's eyes flew open like shutters rising out of control and he spit out the awful paste. Instead of toothpaste he had slathered the brush with Ben Gay.

The memory continued to play over in her mind and the chuckle turned into a giggle, then the giggle into a belly laugh, and Katie had to sit on the top of the toilet to prevent her from peeing on the floor she was laughing so hard. Every time the laughter subsided the vision of her great-uncle's face came to mind and the laughter erupted all over again.

It took her awhile to regain her composure and complete the task of brushing her teeth. With the release of laughter, her body felt light and her mind clear. By the time she finished her nightly regime and slipped into bed her heart and spirits were lighter.

CHAPTER ELEVEN

Julianne, her best friend, called and voiced pleasure with Katie's decision to finally stay home and start the transition toward recovery. Katie told her about some of the strange happenings, and Julianne listened without comment. When Katie asked for her opinion, Julianne simply said "there are many things we don't understand but just need to accept." Julianne acknowledged and reinforced Katie's need to follow her own personal journey. She told her by staying at home and dealing with your past you might find a renewed purpose. It sounds to me like going through your home has helped you to start on the path that will lessen your burden and adjust to things that can no longer be.

Julianne reminded Katie of Joseph, a patient they had cared for as new nurses in the intensive care unit. A lesson neither would ever forget. He was dying of liver disease caused by his drug and alcohol abuse and had been in the unit for over a month.

"Julianne, Do you remember the situation with his sisters and the state of affairs regarding his death? I'll never forget it."

The three of them came from various areas of California. Apparently he was a rebel and had been in and out of jail and rehab from his abuse and they were estranged for over twenty years because of it. Stranger yet was the fact that they pleaded with him to survive and told him they couldn't live without him. Finally I took them aside and explained the disease process and his prognosis but more importantly the need to give him permission to go. Each told him they loved and forgave him. He died thirty minutes later.

"It's so important to call each patient by their name and maintain their identity. All people need to know their life has value, no matter what they have done." The idea that a person is a disease or the number of a room really bothers me and I know it bothers others as well. His situation proved to me that there is definitely a power beyond our understanding and that love survives even if the person doesn't."

The memory of one of their first patients soothed Katie's thoughts just to know someone else identified with that strange situation. It granted her permission to accept the unknown. Katie was not crazy for seeing visions or hearing mystery music, just receptive.

After a dinner of salmon, brown rice and green beans Katie took a hot bath laced with lavender oil. She relaxed and enjoyed the hot steamy soak breathing in peace. She then put on her flannel pajamas, climbed into their bed and tried to sleep. Her conversation with Julianne about Joseph, the haunting memory she experienced and the lullaby played over and over in her mind.

When she couldn't sleep, she got up, went to the computer, and continued her exploration. Being home in the computer room made her slightly uneasy. That, however, disappeared as she again immersed herself into the history of the mountain and pass area.

CHAPTER TWELVE

Katie couldn't even imagine the San Bernardino and Riverside areas in 1862 when the valleys flooded. The reports of artifacts and burial grounds of the native people being washed away were well documented. The rain lasted for six weeks with a constant deluge over a forty-eight-hour stretch. The ragging water engulfed the entire valley, devastated the area, and changed the topography of the land in the low-lying regions.

As Katie continued to study the information, she imagined how people must of felt and their hardship when they moved west. Travel by stagecoach with the wood seats, bumps and rough ride was the only, means of travel in the late 1800s, a lot like the covered wagons when people moved west. Men and women were tough in those days she thought. The stage line ran from Los Angles to the area now known as Beaumont. Indian scouts accompanied the stage to protect its passengers and the cargo. The company used the guides because of their knowledge of the land. The historical figure of Wyatt Earp came up in her reading. He, a reputed driver, worked for the Wells Fargo Stage line around that time. She wondered what the dusty ride wound have been like. Apparently, it provided little comfort. They stopped about every four hours for the passengers to stretch their legs and relieve themselves.

Later, stagecoach travel would be replaced by the railroad. Katie could almost visualize the lines of tracks that snaked west in 1876. It was easy because of the many movies she had watched with her father. With the railroad and stage lines providing greater accessibility to travelers, California expanded at a faster rate, especially when gold was discovered. Unfortunately for the Native Americans, whites overwhelmed their land. Not only did tribes war among themselves but now they fought the white man.

CHAPTER THIRTEEN

Katie found herself emotionally spent after another day of letting go of her husband's belongings. Being home, going through the closets and rooms of her loved ones, made her feel like she just ran a marathon. She knew that she not only needed to release his possessions but the emotional baggage of grief as well. She closed the latest boxes, and as she did, her stomach growled. It was almost seven in the evening and she was hungry. She heated some tomato soup, made herself a grilled cheese sandwich, added a tall glass of milk and sat down at the table.

Now she sat alone in silence where her husband and daughter's, conversation had occupied the entire room. As Katie proceeded with the tasks at hand and time passed she found her emotions became less fragile. She ate the last bite of her sandwich and as she cleared the table, an overwhelming feeling of fatigue swept over her. Katie went to the bathroom, completed her nightly routine, put on her nightgown and got into bed. Amazingly she relaxed and felt sleepy. It didn't take long for her to fall fast asleep.

Dreams with details and situations that related to her research constantly occupied her mind now as she slept. It was almost as if she participated in the past history, but only as an observer. As the territories of California opened, many people moved from the east for the land and to escape the oppressive social restrictions. The old social stigmas would be replaced in time by other more appropriate for the more rugged areas. History had proved that fact true.

Katie wondered if, with her studies, she might be intruding in time or simply passing through history. As she continued, she now understood why some of the names of the surrounding cities, streets, and historical sites were actually tribal names. Yucaipa, a name meaning green valley, came from the Soboba Indians who inhabited the area. Temecula, Idyllwild, Arrowhead, Cajon Pass, Tahquitz, plus numerous names she recalled signified that very fact.

It had been almost a month since she talked herself into staying home longer than a few days. Now after a year of running away, it was time to tackle the emptiness and finally begin to find serenity therein. She started by throwing away all the dead plants. It took a week to clean her entire house from top to bottom.

Another step Katie needed to take would be to change the message on her answering machine. Katie played it just to savor Dan and Casey's voices. It had taken almost an hour to record it. Dan started the recording by saying "You have reached Dan, and then Katie said her name followed by Casey. The rest of the recording is what took time because they tried to say together, "we are not available at this time so please leave a message and we will get back to you as soon as possible." The problem was that they couldn't say it in unison and laughter always erupted. Eventually they got it together and set the recorder. Now Katie chose a prerecorded message with a man's voice so it wouldn't be apparent that she was alone, but she saved the original recording so she could return to it and hear their voices again.

After listening to her new recording, she restocked the ice chest to return again to Silent Glen. I feel an invisible pull and comfort when I'm in the mountains, but I want to do something other than simply exist. Maybe it's time to return to work. It will give me a renewed purpose and nursing is something I dearly love and I worked so hard to get my degree. Maybe it can also preserve my sense of worth.

Katie returned home weekly to collect the mail and make sure everything was okay. With each visit she made more progress with Dan's belongings and a few of Casey's. Now that the pain wasn't as severe, the positive memories flowed like a never-ending river and it was easier to stay at home. "I'm not ready to stay home all the time and my mountain haven still draws me back to discover its secrets." She left around noon. Out of the corner of her eye, she caught a glimpse of a man and a little girl walking hand and hand near the house. It startled her. She slammed on the brakes and twisted around in her seat. She then turned her car around and went back to the house.

* * *

She searched the entire area but found no sign of the pair. Reluctantly she drove away with the renewed felling of loss and a heavy heart. "Maybe they were trying to tell me they were okay."

She stopped to pick up a few things at the store before heading up the hill and when she came out, two children sat just outside the door with a box of kittens. A tiny gray kitten climbed out of the box and made its way to Katie. At that very moment she knew the kitten would be hers. As she lifted the kitten to get a better look, she noticed the fur wasn't totally gray but tipped with silver. It reminded of her of a dark cloud with a silver lining.

The kitten snuggled closer and memories flooded her mind of Casey cuddling with her just before falling asleep. Katie pondered her life and the progress she continued to make in the resolution in her grief. "I'll call you Spirit," Katie said. The name personified her renewed enthusiasm and attitude, her decision to live life without losing the essence of those she lost. She collected the needed items for the kitten, tucked her new friend and companion safely in a small box, and drove up the hill. The family had often discussed getting Casey a pet, but never had.

As Katie continued her journey, she made the decision to return to work. It would offer her a way to make a difference in the lives she touched, a continued tribute to her loved ones. She would call her supervisor in a few days.

Cathie Norton

CHAPTER FOURTEEN

At the RV, she put away all of the groceries and sat staring out the window as the kitten snuggled in her lap. If only she could wish or pray Dan and Casey back to life. I'm hungry, really hungry and got jack cheese and a bunch of red seedless grapes out of the bag of groceries. With each grape she ate she counted her blessings.

The ecstasy of love's first kiss
The joy of falling deeply in love
Dan, her loving husband and best friend
The tenderness of walking hand in hand
Being loved and giving love in return
The feeling of a life inside her body, her daughter
Nurturing a new life by nursing her baby
The pleasure of sharing life as a family
The unconditional gift of love from Casey
The satisfaction and peace of a sleeping child
Christmas morning's tangible excitement
A healthy family
A home filled with love and pleasure
Caring friends and family
A nurturing career
Life in the USA and freedom
Time to grieve
A peaceful place to recover

Joy filled Katie's heart like a waterfall cresting over a drop overflowing the pool below. A multitude of memories tumbled over and over in her mind, too numerous to capture on paper. Tears rolled down her cheeks, tears of joy, not pain, as she counted her blessings. She now found it possible to savor the greatest part of her life as she looked over the list she had made. She realized as she reviewed these highlights of her life, how blessed she was.

With her appetite satisfied, she decided a little exercise would do her good. Katie continued to ponder her good fortune with her renewed perspective. She enjoyed taking care of and sharing time and space with her new friend, her lovely kitten, Spirit. The healing process took time but now she ate routinely, regained the weight she had lost and looked more like her old self. The depression and gigantic weight that once consumed her heart hurt progressively less as she emerged into her new self. Her coach gave her a place to retreat, lick her wounds and regain her sense of well-being while renewing her outlook. It also offered her time to re-establish herself as one instead of part of a threesome.

CHAPTER FIFTEEN

The next morning, even though the day appeared slightly foggy, she decided to drive further up the mountain to Idyllwild. Katie secured Spirit in the bathroom with anything the kitten might need during her absence. Her trip took her past the white sandy rocks along the hillside as she traveled up the mountain. They reminded her of the color of a white-washed fence. How did they get such a smooth surface? Could it be that water had sculpted the hillside? Maybe rain fell over the side of the cliffs etching the present palette.

Katie arrived in the rural town of Idyllwild with its friendly people, some who looked vaguely familiar from previous trips to the area. She studied people with a new perspective. No one she saw had dark skin, high cheek bones or the heavy bone structure she attributed to the Native American population. She wandered aimlessly through the shops, browsing, looking for nothing in particular. She purchased some beef jerky, a variety of herbal tea, a tea pot and a red heart-shaped wind chime with large crystal hearts inside each chime. The gems sparkled in the sunlight like rainbows being chased by butterflies.

It would be nice to have a cup of tea now and again. She rarely drank tea. Dan preferred coffee and she enjoyed the coffee he ground fresh from rich whole beans every morning.

The brochures she received from the grief counselor encouraged "those left behind" to make little changes in order to continue the healing process. Altering where she dined, holiday traditions, or even drinking tea now instead of coffee, would be a start. One by one she would replace some of her past habits and establish new ones. Sharing life with Spirit would begin a new chapter of her life.

The fog lifted slightly when she returned from Idyllwild and, exhausted, she lay on the sofa to rest. The leaves rustling through the trees and sounded like ocean waves and the sound lulled her into a peaceful sleep.

She awoke with a start, feeling someone touching her on the shoulder, only to find she was totally alone. "I swear someone touched me" she told her Spirit who lay on the dash sunning herself. In the distance she heard the same familiar and reassuring lullaby that always comforted her.

She needed to get back to her research to find out more about the area. Katie now recognized without a doubt, that the spirits of the mountain wanted their story told. No longer surprised to see the lovely women, hear the lullaby or flute, she now found peace in the resonances of the trees; their tales. The trees provided a wide-range of soothing sounds. Interesting too, was how many different tones she recognized. At times they resembled the sound of silence and at others the angry turbulence of despair. The loss and wounds of grief, though ever present, were not as raw as they once had been. The mountain seemed to continue provide a healing process.

CHAPTER SIXTEEN

Returning to work would be a challenge. "It is time," Katie told spirit. Taking care of severely ill and injured patients might affect her recovery, but how much? Staying at home or in her motorhome could not last forever and she needed to resume her life.

Katie called Julianne and told her she'd contacted their manager and had scheduled an appointment for the next day. They agreed to meet for lunch and talk about Katie's fears. It would be a few weeks before she could start work; she had to complete the mandatory yearly courses. The time would also give her an opportunity to see how she felt about the return as well as how others reacted to her.

Katie arrived a few minutes before nine to meet with the new manager of the intensive care unit. To her surprise the room was filled with all the staff and auxiliary personnel of the unit. Even the off duty staff were there. A bouquet of pink roses, white daisies, and lavender iris sat on the table and there were breakfast goodies of fresh fruit and croissants as well. Everyone greeted her with warm hugs and told her they missed her, and how pleased they were to know she planned to return to work. Katie's past responsibility had been to provide mentorship to all new nurses when they started in the unit. Her reputation of a well-rounded, knowledgeable, experienced and caring person preceded her. The unexpected, overwhelming greeting surprised her, lifting her spirits and touching her heart.

She made arrangements to meet with the education

department for the required mandatory skills update at the beginning of the next week. Katie now looked forward to her return to the hospital. The warm welcome she received made her realize the staff and her professional friends would now support her as she transitioned back to the bedside.

Julianne met Katie for lunch as planned. Other members of the unit would join them later. They all wanted to hear about her research of the mountain. Julianne omitted personal facts, the ones Katie asked her to keep secrets but had shared what Katie found out about the Indian lore. She had also kept the staff informed about Katie's coping skills and her grief recovery. The research she'd done and discoveries she'd made fascinated them and they wanted to hear more about what she had found.

During lunch she informed the group that the name Poppet Flats came from the family who established their home as a ranch then later on as a farm. She went on to say that on one of her walks around the campsites, she noticed a stone building just behind the youth center and discovered that it had a colorful past. "It served as a trading post, a school house, a general store and a creamery, as well as a bunkhouse for shepherds and cowboys in the early days. During prohibition it produced whisky and flourished. The proprietors of that small rock house made a hefty profit and the building gained the name "Bootlegger's Castle". They all were interested in the tale and eagerly listened. "It's now used as a playhouse for the children."

Katie informed them that when she delved further into the area's history, she found out the area once had a hot springs that were discovered in 1820 by Padre Zalvidea Joaquin Nunez. Then in 1852 the Mormons built a logging road up to the hot springs. A doctor named David Noble Smith purchased the land and established it as retreat for healing because of the minerals in the water, healing powers and the serenity of its location. Later the area would be known as Smiths Hygienic Sanatorium. Katie liked sharing the information with others who were as intrigued by the area's history as was she. She promised to update the group with whatever facts she discovered.

CHAPTER SEVENTEEN

Katie spent less and less time in her mountain retreat once she returned to work. She could live on the insurance money if she so desired but decided not to. She recalled how they had taken out the policy right after they were married. Never in a million years did she imagine the need to use it. Returning to work gave her a renewed sense of purpose as well as a diversion from her loneliness. It also gave her companionship she needed and someone to talk to, and a gift for oneself with interactive conversation. "I worked hard to obtain my nursing degree and I am a good nurse, no, a great nurse;" she told the mirror as she combed her now shiny golden hair.

Initially when she resumed her work, she functioned as a staff nurse in the intensive care unit, but found it emotionally draining in spite of support from the others.

A new position, the title of case manager, was created and she applied for it. It held great possibilities. She would be away from direct patient care but still involved with the staff and patients. She would function as a patient advocate, and help families cope with traumatic and critical situations. Katie always acted on the behalf of the patients and their family anyway. She would be the perfect selection if granted the position.

Katie received the position as the first case manager in the hospital. Her small office, just outside the intensive care unit, would be perfect, granting access to current patient records, staff and families. She decorated her office with excitement, painting the walls pastel green. According to studies on color in nursing school, the soft green color provided a calming, healing effect. On the new shelves she placed a special picture of her family, nursing memorabilia, including her great aunt's scissors set, old glass urine collection bottles which she used to hold wild flowers, her original nursing cap, and an assortment of reference books. She hung her nursing license, her certificates of achievement, and a Norman Rockwell reproduction of a nurse caring for a bedridden child on the wall above her desk. Other walls held a collection of variable-sized old maps. Katie's excitement showed in the change in her demeanor, her renewed enthusiasm, the smile she now sported, and the desire to get to work.

In her new role, she could gather information from the staff and patient charts. This material would provide a greater understanding of tests, procedures and outcomes and she would educate patients and families in laymen's terms. It would free up the doctors, who didn't always explain everything in clear precise terms, and free the nurses to provide more patient care. Other valuable material would come from the nurses. They often would gather facts directly from contact with the patient and family or from nurse to nurse during their report at shift changes. With current data she could assist all concerned in navigating the rigors of hospitalization.

Simply by her caring, knowledge, comprehension of information, and insight into human nature, Katie would provide all she served with facts and insights they could understand. Katie prayed with patients and families, held them when they cried, and by her presence gave them hope or at least solace. The new position was a perfect fit for her and, when appropriate, she would be able to share her own situation and feelings of loss to better connect with those hurting. It would greatly benefit the staff, the patients and family, as well as the hospital. It also helped Katie heal.

CHAPTER EIGHTEEN

After arriving home from a full day at work, she heard a soft knock on the front door. When she opened the door there stood a dark- haired little girl with pigtails, and big, brown cocker-spaniel eyes. The child appeared to be about six years old.

She held out a few sprigs of slightly wilted lilacs. "Hi, my name is Samantha and my friend wanted me to bring these to you because she said you liked these flowers."

Katie gently took the flowers from the child and thanked her. "What is your friends' name?" Katie asked. "I don't know," the little girl said, "she's just my friend." Katie, now intrigued, invited the little girl in but she refused. "I can't go into strangers' houses. I have to go back to my grandmother's house now, but my friend wanted me to tell you she loves you lots and not to cry."

Katie was slightly bewildered but curious. "What does your friend look like?"

Samantha grinned broadly exposing a missing left front tooth and said "her eyes are really-really blue; she has almost white hair and she's an angel". She went on to say that her friend, the angel, visited her at the foot of her bed when she felt sad that her parents were gone so often and before she fell asleep at night. "My angel said she has a treasure chest with fancy grown-up clothes in it." Samantha stood a little taller with her hands outstretched and her body vibrating with excitement as she described Casey's favorite dress up outfit. "Her favorite dress in her treasure chest is the red one with sparkles all over it and the feathers she likes best are the yellow ones."

Samantha told Katie that her father traveled a lot and her mother worked at night, so she stayed with her grandmother who lives down the street. Samantha said she had to go and Katie gave her a big hug and thanked her for the flowers. She told the little girl she would like to hear more about her friend. "Sam, everyone calls me Sam," she said, waving goodbye as she skipped down the street with her pigtails bobbing up and down.

As Katie closed the door and leaned against it, her mind spun as she tried hard to absorb what Sam told her. She held the wilted flowers against her breast and savored their fragrance. She pondered the miracle of a child's innocence and the simple acceptance of what they perceived as fact. It brought with it a warm feeling, and tenderly carried Casey's love closer to Katie's soul. She allowed herself to absorb the impact of Sam's message, being able to hear "I love you" from Casey.

It was then she noticed the leather-bound book on the dining room table, the one the old woman had given her. She picked it up and cradled it, stroking it as if it were her child. The leather was soft and silky, just like Casey's hair.

Katie made her way to the living room, sat in Dan's recliner and opened the book. On the front page, when she recalled the previously blank sheets, there were the words. "Where you were lost, now you are found." Was she crazy, seeing and hearing things, and now words magically materializing on paper? She believed those who died looked after and protected persons left behind. "I never thought I would be the recipient of that heavenly gift."

The photo albums caught Katie's eye. She picked up the third of the series of eight, and opened it. There, staring up at her, were her daughter's sky-blue eyes. Casey stood with the ocean in the background. The close-up revealed a slightly sandy little girl, and alongside her father with a half built sand castle. For three summers they had rented a home for a week in Newport Beach. Katie closed her eyes and was immediately transported back in time.

She could feel the brisk tantalizing breeze against her skin, cooling the warmth of the sun. Katie heard the irregular pulsation of the waves as they peaked just before they caressed the shore. She could almost taste the salt in the air. She could see the reflective blue of the ocean waves just before they curled into frothy white foam; the image always soothed her and was one she dearly loved. She lovingly remembered how the grains of sand felt between her toes, and massaged her feet as she walked at the edge of the frothy action.

Katie's mind replayed walking hand-in-hand with her and Dan, swinging Casey between them, as they strolled along the water's edge. "Yes, a magical time, and one that will always be part of me even if they won't." She opened her eyes and smiled at the gifts she had been given and would keep forever.

The memories continued to play over and over in her mind. Casey loved Balboa; they rode their bikes and took the ferry over, then stopped for ice cream, Casey's favorite part. Their preferred place for lunch at Charley's Chile was in Newport Beach, just off the pier. Established in 1969, it served meals all day, but it was the chili they all enjoyed most. Katie could almost taste it.

Early on weekend mornings, as the fishing boats arrived directly from the sea, they bought fresh fish from the Dory fleet and they always managed to take a few selections home to enjoy later- Casey's selections.

A stop at the Crab Cooker on their way home at the end of their vacation was part of their tradition. Dan loved the fact that the restaurant made President Nixon wait for a table just like everyone else. Casual dining with plastic silverware and checked red table cloths didn't detract from the famous clam chowder, scrumptious scallops, shrimp and fish; the taste always unbeatable.

Katie placed the albums back on the shelf and wandered aimlessly, ending up in her bedroom. There she realized nothing had changed since they moved into the house five years earlier. They'd purchased the heavy mahogany furniture and accented the room with light blue paint and sheer white drapes. The sandy-beige chenille bedspread they chose was accented by throw pillows in shades of blue that rested on the bed. Dan always complained that he had to remove all the pillows before he could climb into bed.

"It's time for a transformation" Katie said. The decision made, she went shopping. "First I need to find a new comforter set. I don't want to get rid of the blue paint, but simply to change the atmosphere of room the a bit."

At the third store, she found the perfect spread. The pattern reminded Katie of an artist's sketch with fine-lined etchings. It had flowers and leaves outlined with charcoal and accented with pastel and medium shades of blue, pale sage green, silver and gray. Accompanying it were matching lined drapery panels, a valance, and pillow shams. Along with the drapes she found shimmering silver sheers to replace the white ones on the window. She could keep the wall color and highlight the room with the sage green and grays. As she neared the counter she located two crystal side lamps with silver shades and added them to her purchase.

"I'll take the old bedspread from our room to the RV and change out the comforter that came with the coach. I'll start with my bedroom then progress to the other rooms. Maybe I'll do the kitchen next." As she thought about it she became more excited.

The kitchen had black granite counter tops with copper flecks throughout and the walls were white. She had copper accessories but now it needed something else. "I know. I'll accent it with red, maybe in an apple motif" she said out loud as if sharing the idea with someone else.

Katie contemplated the changes she planned to make and the realization came to her, this is the transition the grief counselor described.

She looked down at her wedding ring set. I don't want to take it off but maybe it is part of the evolution. "I know" she said, "I'll have the diamonds made into a necklace. Our home town jeweler is creative and the heart-shaped diamond can be the focal point. He can use the other stones to surround the center stone. It will make a beautiful necklace. This way it will always be close to my heart. I can wear the oval opal ring grandpapa gave me for my sixteenth birthday on that finger so it won't feel so vacant and lonely. I've always loved that large fiery oval ring with the tiny rose gold flowers on each side. I haven't worn it since Daniel gave me my engagement ring." Katie sighed but knew change was inevitable but growth was optional. She needed to grow not just exist. "It's time."

Cathie Norton

CHAPTER NINETEEN

After Katie's return to work and the career she prized, and her study of the mountain's history slowed but she went to the computer as often as she could. She found the native people continued their rituals, in attempt to prevent further natural catastrophes such as earthquakes, floods, poor fishing, and failed crops. Traditional ceremonies are still practiced yearly at the powwows with many tribes gathered to celebrate. She remembered advertisements that welcomed visitors to the event, and a few in her group had attended the powwows. They reported the historical attire and musical instruments that graced the Indians participate in the event and represent their ancestors during the celebration.

A thought came to her like a lightning bolt. Her voyage from grief to hope and purpose somewhat resembled that of the Native American journey. Once they were intact with joy and prosperity, then they made their way through despair, hardship and pain, to again regain resolution and hope. Katie smiled and she wondered when she had last smiled. Then she remembered one of her favorite poems from her childhood, written by an unknown author.

Happiness is like a butterfly.
If pursued, is just beyond your reach.
But if you sit down quietly, may alight upon you.

Katie believed that things happen for a reason and purpose

to serve and teach us lessons. It had been impossible to fathom why Dan and Casey died. "I may never know until I ask the Lord in heaven but there has to be a reason," she told Julianna over lunch one day. "Maybe he needed our Casey to return to heaven to inspire others." Then Katie shared Sam's visit and the impact that gave her unbelievable peace.

"As I continue my studies of Silent Glen, the native people and the unusual experiences I'm having, it may give me a slight glimpse as to the purpose. I'd rather not have lost my family but I didn't have a choice."

CHAPTER TWENTY

With the weekend off Katie decided to travel to Idyllwild for the day. She always hiked up past the base of Lunch Rock closer to Lily Rock since she unearthed the story of the couple to pay homage. To honor them she placed flowers. This time, to her amazement, a large portion of the rock that covered the entrance had eroded away, probably due to age and the pressure of the massive weight of the gigantic boulders. It left a large gap between the rocks that surrounded the boulder. Because of its sacred nature as a burial site, she did not venture inside. Instead she returned to Idyllwild and contacted the Cultural Center Research Library at the Soboba Indian reservation. There she reported her findings. Representatives from the Soboba and Cahuilla Nation council of elders returned to the area with Katie. She remained outside curious as to what they found. She as an outsider knew she would not be welcome.

The elders quarantined off the area and a larger portion of the eroded rock so they could excavate farther to expose the inside of the cave. They told her the cave revealed an enormous expanse and would take weeks or even years to explore. A few weeks later Katie received a call. The chief, Rising Waters, reported success. They found the couple inside. Two mummified bodies, embracing, were located in a hollowed out area deep in the cave. The decayed clothes, from the appropriate time period, further added credence to the story of the lovers. The tribesmen and shaman reverently wrapped the couple in a hand-made Native American blanket as a spiritual chant encircled the workers like smoke from a fire; they then placed them in a carved wooden box and transported them to their sacred burial site.

The elder of the tribe explained that the burial ritual started with a wake that lasted all night, where songs and chants were offered to their ancestors. These would assist the couple in their travel to the next world. Then the burning of clothing would take place. The only piece available was a piece of the man's vest, both of his moccasins, and one of hers. Because the bodies had become one, no other clothing could be obtained; it would disturb their travel to the great beyond. Their traditions welcomed the couple and guaranteed their passage to the next life so they would always walk together. The internment rituals continued at one of the tribal cemeteries. The loving couple received high honors from the tribe and were buried, rejoining their long-departed ancestors.

Katie felt honored to be selected to witness sections of the ceremonies. Other parts were restricted to only specific members of the tribe. After the burial, she placed a bouquet of wild flowers on the grave and wished the couple a good life in the thereafter together. Now they could rest and find peace and harmony surrounded by their ancestors. Katie continued to be thankful for the gift and comfort provided by the long lost princess. She too, felt a sense of tranquility and healing having experienced the completion of their story and the beginning of hers.

CHAPTER TWENTY-ONE

When Katie arrived home, Spirit, her now full-grown cat, greeted her at the door. Her companion weaved in and out between her legs, purring as she lovingly massaged Katie's lower legs with her soft fur. Katie previously had given her cat a pink collar with a tiny silver bell. It allowed her to know where her friend was at all times. They often played hide and seek, but Katie could always find her; the bell gave her away.

It amazed others that the cat loved to ride in the car. She always knew when they would visit Silent Glen; she meowed and paced at the door ready to go. Spirit loved to lie on the dash of their RV to sun herself.

Having the responsibility of the cat gave Katie a sense of comfort. Her friend and companion slept with her and lay in her lap to offer unconditional love and affection. Katie missed her family and continued to feel the loss but her feline companion made her happy. The cat seemed to know instinctively when Katie needed more of her attention and feistiness to comfort a hectic day or a melancholy mood.

Spirit perched herself on top of the computer console as Katie continued her research. It was almost as if the cat's interest was piqued by the history as well.

Cathie Norton

CHAPTER TWENTY-TWO

Julianne convinced Katie to attend their fifteen-year high school reunion. Julianne's husband was God knew-where as he fulfilled his military duty. Julianne told Katie she had received letters, filtered through the ranks, to hide the fact Ben had been deployed to somewhere secret. The only way Julianne would attend their reunion was if her best friend Katie would go with her. They could be one another's escort. Julianne told Katie it would be good for her to get back into a more social life other than work.

Katie's mood had lightened since she returned to work, but she still continued to be reserved in any social setting. No longer angry with God, she attended church regularly and continued to search for the reason he had taken away her family. The choir director approached her after church one day and asked her to join the choir. They needed sopranos and he knew she sang first soprano, something the choir needed desperately. She had, once enjoyed singing and he knew song gave someone the ability to express emotion in a positive way. Katie pondered the request then happily agreed.

Katie joined Julie and the group of three military wives who had all attended the same high school, but other than that she didn't go out socially. The group of four women initiated lunch dates and rallied to support Katie after Daniel's and Casey's deaths. They all had something in common: distant loved ones with constant loneliness in their lives. Two years had passed and the anniversary of Dan's and Casey's death still hurt and always would. Julianne felt that the reunion would take Katie's mind off the occasion, even if only briefly.

The four women picked Katie up at her home to shop in Palm Springs, have lunch, then more shopping. Dinner was planned at The Falls, a well-known restaurant that served smoking martinis, and a selection of unique appetizers such as crab-stuffed mushrooms, deep fried artichoke hearts, and hand-fed beef, all gourmet items. Julianne almost had to hog-tie Katie in order to get her to go, but knew once they all got together she would be fine. They all could benefit with the war escalating after 9-11.

Ben, Julianne's husband, had been employed at Cal State San Bernardino as a professor. He taught creative writing, and multiple languages when the "military action" was declared. He immediately signed up to work with the Department of Defense as an interpreter for the Army. In a way, the excuse to go shopping kept the minds of the wives "off that dreaded letter." They all knew it could arrive at any time to inform them of the death of their husband.

August 15th was the date for their high school reunion, and the site, the Newport Beach Country Club. Each graduate received a survey to highlight significant events since graduation. Daniel graduated two years ahead of Katie so many of her classmates knew him. When Katie returned her form she did not mention his or their daughter's death. Julianne, however, informed the reunion board. They could share the information with their classmates to hopefully lessen the pain of others asking about Dan.

CHAPTER TWENTY-THREE

The sun shone bright as the five ladies headed toward their destination, their first stop Palm Canyon Drive. None intended to purchase items there, but wanted the experience of strolling in and out of the expensive boutiques.

"I want to try on the most expensive dresses they have" exclaimed one of the women. This would give each of them great ideas when they did purchase their outfits for the reunion.

They planned to stop by Starbucks on the way for coffee and a croissant, and then proceed into each and every shop before they stopped for lunch.

Katie stayed quiet, and less enthusiastic then the other four gals, but as they traveled in the car toward their destination, her mood brightened. It would be fun to regain more joy in her life. Her time at Silent Glen and her haunting glimpses into the past now gave her a different perspective of life and death.

She felt less empty since she returned to work and now found a new completeness in herself. With all the chatter and excitement that surrounded the upcoming reunion, she relaxed and delighted in herself in the here and now. She enjoyed the breeze that filtered through her hair and the laughter of the others. One never knew how long life would last, but now, acutely aware of that fact, she needed to build upon the gifts she had been given. Katie allowed herself to find joy in the friendship of the other women and to plan for her future. It gave her great satisfaction.

She knew those she loved were in heaven and it was she who

had suffered. In the last two years the agony eased and she had discovered more about herself. They married during the second year of college so she really hadn't discovered her inner talent and strength.

The group ate lunch at the Blue Coyote, and enjoyed the special of the day, tacos and tequila. They relaxed and the conversation intensified as they finished their margaritas. Stomachs full they were now eager to discover just the right outfit. One by one each found the ideal dress, shoes, and accessories, and all before dinner. Dinner at the Falls restaurant provided entertainment as they watched the dry ice in the martinis rise like smoke. Katie and the other gals giggled at the sight and reminisced about the antics of their high school days. "Remember the math teacher Miss White? One of the boys placed a mouse in her desk and we could hear her scream all over campus". This sent the entire group into another set of giggles. Katie couldn't help but remember other situations of pranks.

As Katie sat back, she felt a sense of continued contentment. She had begun to feel more accustomed to her single life, without regrets, and no longer angry with God and Dan. "I married an extremely loving man and my best friend." She thought. Katie sighed as memories flooded her mind with the warmth of a soft blanket. It reminded her of a dream come true. Many never knew the amazement of that kind of relationship. Together they loved Casey, a part of each of them, their own flesh and blood. Alive she couldn't have been more perfect, and was now truly an angel. What a privilege to experience the greatest gift one could imagine, their child. She sighed deeply, glad she had agreed to go shopping with her friends and attend the reunion.

Returning home, she climbed her stairs and opened her front door. Katie again heard the lullaby and serenity bathed her, knowing that the princess found harmony with her mate and people. Maybe her music signified a final goodbye to Katie? Maybe it wished her peace as well?

CHAPTER TWENTY-FOUR

The day of the reunion rapidly arrived and Katie and Julianne sat in the beauty shop enjoying their manicure and pedicure. Next they would indulge in an entire body massage, and then later have their hair done. A day of pampering would be relished and well-deserved.

"I don't remember the last time I took time to do anything for myself" exclaimed Katie.

The ladies arranged for a room at the Marriott Hotel. The entire weekend would be theirs and they would head out later that morning. Their clothes were all packed and their excitement heightened.

They delighted in a few pre-reunion events at one of the local hot spots earlier that month, meeting old classmates. Katie couldn't get over how some had changed very little and others no one would recognize unless they announced who they were. The occasional whisper arose from the classmates who were still single and match-making abounded.

Katie continued to be amazed when told she hadn't changed at all over the last fifteen years. "I look in the mirror daily and see some of my mother: she thought. It brought a smile to her face, but more importantly to her eyes. She glanced over at Julianne, who recognized that tell-tale look. The look that said it pleased her. "You know me so well," Katie said.

The girls drove in Julianne's convertible with the top down scarves securely tied to minimize the damage to their hair-dos. Katie's mind wandered as they got into the car. It was a beautiful day to start their adventure. Her more-casual hair style gave Katie's short, natural curly hair an advantage; it would be easier to manage after the long ride. Upon arriving, they checked into their rooms and put their things away, before going down for lunch beside the pool. They enjoyed a glass chardonnay with their shrimp cocktail. They sat basking in the warmth of the afternoon sun. It provided relaxation and offered the opportunity to add a little color to their otherwise pale bodies before they dressed for the event that evening. Katie remembered fondly the gift of time to "just relax" when a five-year-old wanted to be entertained.

Katie and Julianne entered the Country Club to register for the event. A wolf whistle came from the side line and both girls jumped and looked in the direction from whence it came.

"Wow, don't you gals look terrific," said the strikingly attractive man. "Remember me? I'm Jake." Katie and Julianne looked at each stunned.

Katie answered slightly embarrassed, "Yes I do, but in high school you were short and pudgy."

"I'm a late bloomer" Jake said. He stood about six feet tall with a sculptured body and wore a tailored gray pinstripe suit.

"Wow what a transformation," They said in unison. He escorted them to the registration table then excused himself.

The group at the table greeted the two women with complements.

"Katie, you look like a fairy princess" one said.

Katie's petite hour glass body accented the shimmering aqua gown to perfection. The color reminded Katie of the Western Caribbean water and Dan. Initially she thought the slightly low-cut bodice revealed too much but decided it would be fine for the evening. Her mother's pearls and drop earrings were a perfect accent to the gown. "I'm glad I regained the weight I lost after Dan and Casey's death," she told Julianne. "I'm about the same weight as in high school."

In contrast to Katie's petite body, Julianne's lanky slender figure accented the sleek silver gown with a slit up the side of the pencil skirt.

"You remind me of a tall willowy birch tree, elegant and graceful" Katie told her.

The small ruby and diamond necklace and earrings that were a gift from Ben further accented her outfit and a thought came to Katie's mind of a wintery Christmas.

"Julianne, you look amazing," Katie had told her when they had left the hotel for the event. Katie and Julianne shared a look of contentment as they left and received nods of approval from all they passed.

Each table seated eight and the group of five women planned to sit together but no single table was available, so they split up.

"I'm disappointed we can't all be together during dinner," Katie said.

She and Julianne found themselves sitting with people they didn't remember from school, basically total strangers. It didn't surprise either of them; their class graduated over five hundred.

Katie and Julianne were fascinated by the outrageous claims, the others made about their achievements and status. They listened, nodded with amusement at each other and smiled. Because they had been friends for years they could almost read one another's mind.

Julianne whispered in Katie's ear. "What a crock of shit" she said. They both laughed but the others didn't notice.

The dinner of prime rib, which melted in your mouth, was superb. Each table held two carafes of wine, one red and one white. They limited themselves to a glass, but the rest was consumed readily by the other guests. With dinner and dessert over, the rest of the group made their way to the bar and were never seen again. Katie and Julie met with the other three ladies but as the evening progressed they all went their own separate ways.

The dancing began and the sight of couples embracing, overwhelmed Katie, so she stepped outside to watch the calm water of the bay. Water always provided a soothing effect for her. She had told and retold the story of Daniel and their daughter's death and it made her weary. "If I have to tell it one more time I'll scream" she thought. As she found her way to the dimly lit area of the patio, tears spilled from her eyes. Having repeated Dan and Casey's death made her miss them all the more. The second anniversary of their death also weighed heavily on her even though the night provided a diversion. She wondered what it would have been like if Dan still lived and they had come to the reunion together. Her thoughts were miles away as she stared unseeingly at the water.

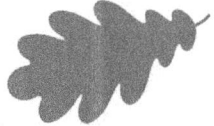

CHAPTER TWENTY-FIVE

Katie stood in the dark and didn't notice the man enter the patio. He stood just to her right and carefully inched closer as she began to regain her composure.

He cleared his throat as a warning sign and she looked in his direction.

Due to the dim light and encroaching fog from the bay, she couldn't clearly see him. His voice was soothing and as he approached, he handed her his handkerchief and spoke gently and asked, "Are you all right."

She acknowledged with an affirming nod of her head in his direction but didn't move.

He had come out to get some fresh air and found that her emotion overwhelmed him as well. He stood quietly beside her as they gazed out over the bay. Katie handed him back his handkerchief and he placed a hand on her arm to reassure her. "Would you like to talk about it?" he said.

It surprised her that a stranger asked her to share something so painful as to bring her to tears.

She glanced his way and in the dim moonlight saw tears inching down his cheeks. Katie didn't know if his tears were for her, but reflected his own pain. He stood leaning on the rail stooped over slightly, so she couldn't tell his height. Katie didn't pull her arm away. She sighed and enjoyed the warmth of another human being.

He spoke softly with a strangled voice. "I lost my wife in New York. She was in the World-trade Center when the first plane hit" he said.

"I lost my husband and daughter in a fiery crash in the Cajon Pass."

They stood in silence, and then he gently took her hand while they were both immersed in their own thoughts.

Time passed and then the party moved from the inside to the patio. Other voices interrupted the silence, but more so, the intimacy of sharing something so personal and profound.

"My name is Harold" he said.

She told him, "I'm Katie."

"Would you like to dance?"

She nodded in agreement and he escorted her to the dance floor. Even though the light was dim, it was brighter than the patio and provided the opportunity to see one another clearly.

Harold stood almost six feet tall with a slender build, fawn-brown hair, and startling blue eyes. They moved together slowly and just allowed themselves to be alive. He held her close enough to dance, but so close as to make her uncomfortable.

"Do you like to dance?" Harold asked.

Katie nodded but said little, she continued to try to absorb the situation.

As the evening progressed and the crowd thinned, she and Harold found a quiet corner. The main hall had a noise level that reverberated off the walls and echoed in their ears. The quiet gave them an opportunity to share a little more about themselves, although neither said anything.

"I practice law with two other lawyers in San Bernardino and live in Lake Arrowhead,"

Katie told him she worked as a registered nurse at the county hospital. Katie further explained she had been a nurse for twelve years, got her degree from San Bernardino Valley College then obtained her advanced degree at Cal State San Bernardino.

Harold looked surprised. "You look too young to be a nurse, especially for that long!"

Time seemed to pass quickly and soon her classmates informed her they planned to continue their party at one of the local hot spots.

Julianne asked Katie, "would it bother you if I joined them? Would you like to go?"

Katie declined her offer and encouraged her to have fun. "I'll take a cab back to the hotel, just be careful," Katie said.

The Country Club closed at two in the morning, so Katie invited Harold to continue their conversation in the lobby of her hotel. She didn't want to give him the wrong idea and invite him up to the room.

Harold smiled broadly and answered quickly. "I'd be delighted to share the rest of the evening, no, morning with you."

Katie said, "I don't know anyone else who understands loss like you do, plus I enjoy your company."

They took a cab back to the Marriott and found a quiet corner to continue their conversation.

Katie listened as Harold expounded on his feelings. "When Gloria, my wife, died I had no body to bury so it blurred my reality. It took me a long time to even stop looking for her to come through the door. Then one day it hit me. I'll never see her again. It's taken me three years to regain a sense of hope and be comfortable in my own skin."

Katie knew the feeling well. "I felt the same way. I'm just now finding my way as one instead of three."

Their conversation meandered through numerous subjects: childhood, their professions, even religion and politics, usually forbidden subjects.

Katie hesitated to tell him the story of the lullaby and the comfort it provided her until they were talking about unusual things that happened in their lives.

Harold told her about a time shortly after they were married when he was awakened with an overwhelming feeling of dread. "A frigid mist started at my feet and crept up my legs and slowly made its way up to my torso. As it got to my hips I knew without a doubt, that if I didn't stop it and move it totally away from our home, it would smother me and probably my wife. I've never concentrated so hard in my life to focus my energy, especially on something abstract. I mentally moved the icy blanket off my body, out the door and down the street. Then, with my concentrated thoughts, I placed a protective shield, like a bubble, over Gloria and me, then our home. Only then did I know I could return to sleep, and felt no further fear or apprehension."

Katie sat transfixed and intrigued and amazed by his story.

He described it as if it were plot in a scary movie, as the black mist of evil engulfed the unsuspecting couple in a horror film.

"Wow how frightening," is all Katie could say almost breathless.

Katie took his hand, conveying with her touch, that she understood his out of the ordinary experience. "It must have scared you almost to death knowing you could have died." She now felt comfortable enough to share her journey as she escaped to her motor home. "I had an overwhelming emptiness, a hollowness that wasn't visible but nevertheless ever-present after my family died. I heard the lightest whisper through the trees outside our coach. Then the sound of a soft lullaby started and progressed to an undeniable presence. Later I discovered it to be a princess who had been captured and entombed in a cave."

Harold sat, elbows on his knees and nodded with understanding, intensively listening. It surprised them both when the room grew light and the sun came up. "May I call on you some time and maybe get together for dinner?" he asked.

She hadn't planned to date or become close to any man but their shared experiences provided a sense of comfort and deep understanding. Maybe they could be friends?

CHAPTER TWENTY-SIX

Katie entered the hotel room just as the sun started sending ribbons of light through the blinds. She undressed and went to bed as Julianne slept soundly. Katie awoke around ten in the morning when the racket in the room roused her from a sound sleep.

As the fog in her head cleared she heard Julianne on the phone. As the excitement in her voice grew so did its pitch.

"Ben's coming home on leave for Christmas. He's coming home," Julianne shouted, hugging Katie and danced her around the room. "That's great, how long can he stay?" Katie asked. It surprised Katie when Julianne jumped up and down on Katie's bed like a little kid. They again hugged and cried tears with the unexpected joyful news. "I'm starved, let's get dressed and go down for breakfast," Julianne said with a Cheshire cat grim. Ben coming home is the best gift I ever got and he will be stationed in the USA now."

Over breakfast of lox and bagels, Katie took time to share her news. "I met a man who understands my journey and the emotions I've been through. He lost his wife on 9-11. We talked into the morning and he asked if I'd like to go to dinner with him sometime." Katie watched Julianne nod and respond with a twinkle in her eyes. She knew Julianne intently was listening when as a knowingly broad smile crossed her face. Apparently her friend had a little too much drink when she returned after being out with her friends.

Julianne told her she had noticed Katie in deep conversation, but didn't really see who she was with.

"I'm so glad I agreed to come to the reunion with you," Katie said. Katie promised to give her updates on her new friend. She knew, because of their close friendship, that Julianne hoped it would be a fresh beginning. After breakfast they sat by the pool enjoying the rest of the day. They savored the warmth of the sun, fresh crisp air and their continued supportive friendship.

Reservations were set for dinner at the Rusty Pelican. She and Julianne enjoyed a bottle of zinfandel with their steak-Diane and continued the conversation of the events of the previous evening. Katie further enlightened her about Harold and Julianne told her about the excitement she experienced and the amazing clubs the group of friends visited.

The next day they checked out of the hotel. "Hey, let's go shopping." Katie said surprising Julianne.

This again brought an immediate smile to Julianne's face and she laughed out loud. "Sounds great to me" she said. "I want to see if Jared Jewelers can transform my wedding set into something else."

Julianne noticed that Katie wore a different ring on her left hand as they dressed for the dance.

"It is a ring that has an amazing fire opal my grandfather gave me for my sixteenth birthday. I hope my wedding set with its large heart-shaped diamond can be made into a pendant so I can wear it on a chain around my neck. I thought it was time I stopped wearing my wedding rings, don't you?" She asked Julianne.

"Yes absolutely, I was wondering when you would come to that conclusion."

CHAPTER TWENTY-SEVEN

The next month stayed extremely busy at the hospital. The flu bug hit the hospital hard and Katie stayed, worked overtime and worked doubles, sixteen hour shifts, at least three times a week. To add to the hectic schedule, a bus accident on the 10 freeway near Mentone placed the hospital on triage mode and Katie took charge of the evaluation of the arriving patients and the availability of the facility beds. That meant that people were discharged home or transferred to lower-level faculties. This enabled the trauma facilities to accommodate those more seriously injured.

The patients were divided among local hospitals. As trauma centers, the County hospital and Loma Linda University Hospital received nine patients each. Saint Bernadine's got six, and San Bernardino Community Hospital two patients. As things calmed down, with all patients evaluated and appropriate measures taken, Katie yawned and massaged her lower back. She felt overwhelmingly fatigued.

"Boy, I'm tired," she told the unit nurse and she looked it. Her uniform had wrinkles from transporting patients and her normally bouncy step, slower. Her role as a patient advocate continued in spite of the situation and she met with families to keep them updated on their loved ones condition. She also coordinated information from the other hospitals and shared facts and specifics aiding the other facilities.

As Katie was about to leave the unit after eighteen hours on duty, a man burst through the ICU doors, loudly demanding to see his wife. Katie calmly ushered him to the women's bedside and attempted to calm him with her soothing voice.

He showed signs of extreme distress in the tightness of his body language, his red face and the perspiration on his brow. He flailed his arms and shouted incoherently. He definitely demonstrated signs of an inability to think straight.

"She's over here and not injured badly" Katie calmly said, but the man appeared not to hear her.

His wife had sustained numerous abrasions on her face and a few sutured lacerations, and a fractured left arm, with multiple breaks. The woman's arm had a splint in place because she had not yet been to surgery. The hospital policy demanded the more critical patients were to be taken care of first so Katie explained the need for his wife's surgery to be postponed.

Out of the blue the man pulled out a gun, pointed it at Katie and demanded to see the doctor. "Get me the doctor!" he yelled in no uncertain terms.

Katie recoiled, wide eyed with a shocked look on her face and took a step backwards. She then took a deep breath, composed herself then returned to her previous position facing the man. "I'll see if he is available, but you need to calm down," she said firmly with authority.

The man stood by the bedside and his wife spoke softly, took the gun from her husband's shaking hand, and handed it to Katie. She told him she didn't have pain and could easily wait her turn in surgery.

The man took a deep breath, dropped into the nearby chair and started to sob.

The staff later discovered that the gun was not loaded; in fact it was only a replica.

Katie calmly escorted the now-deflated man to her office after he visited with his wife and she patiently listened to his troubles.

"Your wife will receive the absolute best of care and hopefully she can go home in a few days."

Apparently the couple had argued prior to her boarding the bus and he felt guilty. He confessed that it was entirely his fault and that he loved his wife dearly.

"What's your name and how long have your been married," she asked. Katie always tried to make any contact more personal, especially in highly charged situations.

It wasn't uncommon to have someone take out their wrath on a member of the staff instead of their loved one. Katie saw it happen frequently, but not to this extent. "Boy, I'll never forget this," she thought as she sighed deeply.

Hospital security notified the police but Katie said. "Why don't we give him some time to recover from his scare?" When the officer arrived, she encouraged him not to press charges.

The policeman agreed after a long conversation with the man and as he watched how Katie handled the entire, obviously stressful event.

George, the patient's husband, agreed to attend counseling in order to handle his emotions in a more constructive manner and avoid going to jail.

He signed the consent for his wife's surgery and Katie sat with him during the operation. He continued to pour out his heart, saying "I started the argument because I wanted her to spend time with me instead of going with the girls to the outlet mall and I feel stupid for my actions."

"I know that guilty feeling" Katie said. "I lost my husband and little girl and felt guilt-ridden for not being with them."

Her statement connected, his shoulders relaxed and he thanked her for sharing her story.

The police officer stayed behind just in case George because violent again. Katie called and arranged with the hospital psychologist for an appointment for the next day.

George agreed to keep the appointment in order to avoid being arrested. After his wife returned to the unit from surgery and he saw she was alright, he went home.

Cathie Norton

CHAPTER TWENTY-EIGHT

When Katie got home, she fell into bed, not bothering to undress, and was almost asleep before her head hit the pillow. The next day she scanned the mail briefly and saw the light on her message machine blinking. With her hectic work schedule, there had been little time to check it for messages. "I'll check my messages tomorrow, read the mail today." It took her over an hour to scan the snail mail, and another two hours to review her email.

After working sixteen days straight, and weeks of chaos, she now had time off. "All I need is a few days away from work and a week's worth of sleep," she said out loud as if reassuring herself. Her greatest desire would be uninterrupted sleep and time to catch up with her life.

The next morning Katie awoke before nine refreshed the phone rang as she headed to the kitchen to make tea. "Hello" she said in a drowsy voice. It was Harold. Katie apologized. "I'm so sorry I didn't call you back, I listened to my messages before I went to bed, and didn't feel it appropriate to call so late."

Harold explained "I had become concerned when you didn't return my call. I thought maybe you weren't interested in continuing our friendship. I knew you were busy, but then the newspaper carried the story of the flu epidemic, the bus accident and a situation, not specified, at a local hospital. He said the report emphasized the burden it had placed on all of the hospitals and clinics in the area."

Katie reassured Harold. "I'm all right, just a little tired, but better now that I slept all night," Katie said.

They talked comfortably while she prepared, then drank her tea. "Are you available to join me for dinner anytime soon?" he asked.

Katie agreed, a little nervous, because she hadn't dated since Dan, courted her. That's thirteen or so years ago, she thought. "I plan to return to Silent Glen for a few days, but I will be available within a week of two, if that's OK?"

"Sounds great to me, it's a date," Harold said with an enthusiasm that was transmitted through the phone.

They agreed to meet at the Castaway Restaurant a week from Friday night around seven. They sighed in union with relief.

Harold confessed, "I really enjoyed our conversation; our similar but different circumstances and the journey and recovery from a traumatic loss. It feels great to enjoy a female's companionship. I have been apprehensive about dating, it's been so long and things have changed," he told her. His friends were constantly bugging him to get back in the swing of things. "Nothing had been farther from my mind until I met you. You make me feel relaxed and reassured, you're easy to talk to and not demanding or pushy," Harold shared.

"I too have worried about what it would be like to date again and not really knowing if and when I would be ready to start, so I know how you feel," Katie said with a sigh.

CHAPTER TWENTY-NINE

Silent Glen personnel agreed to set up the RV in her favorite spot. The oak trees gave the area a sense of seclusion and the outcropping of multi-tiered rocks lay just to the left past the picnic table. She brought out her laptop and rested it on the table in the coolness of the shade. The computer enabled her to review the research she had done at home. The fascination of "the tale of the trees" hadn't ebbed since the ceremony for the princess; it possessed an almost hypnotic draw. Katie continued her studies, more slowly now, and enjoyed sharing the tidbits of information she collected with the group at the hospital.

According to the most recent information, the era of the gold rush inflicted further devastation on the Native Americans with reports of mass murder. Indians referred to the yellow metal, as "very bad medicine" and it reportedly destroyed all who searched for it. The consequences were catastrophic; resulting from the influx of a hundred thousand adventurers that over-ran the land. The area where the gold miners searched, a reign of terror ensued. In the first two years, the Native American populations sustained a staggering loss of two-thirds of all tribal members. Also documented was the fact that many individual tribes were entirely eradicated.

Katie had a small group that followed with continued interest in any new facts she unearthed. She shared with them the fact that over the time the white man attempted to totally exterminate the Native American population of California.

Katie merged onto the freeway, traveled to meet with the gals for lunch. On the side of the freeway's new retaining wall, she noticed an odd imprinted pattern. It was on the right side of the freeway just before the Wabash off-ramp as she headed west traveling from Yucaipa to Redlands. "I wonder what that is all about." To her it looked like a spider that had been squashed.

After an enjoyable lunch full of laughter she arrived home and went to her computer to investigate the strange design. The reference she found stated that the image originated from Indian folklore and represented the birth of the universe. It went on to say that the tale reportedly was passed down from generation to generation and committed to memory. Their history, in story form, provided security and continued to be ingrained in the tribe's memories so that it would last throughout time. The imprint now exemplified that story. The original pictograph that experts studied appeared to be prehistoric. The artifact, the same image had been found on remnants of pottery and other artifacts. The symbol continued to be used as a solstice position marker.

"Wow, the unique art on the concrete had a significant meaning to the area after all."

After she returned to Silent Glen, she continued her course of study, the way her native brothers and sisters were treated throughout the early history of California upset her.

She shared her frustrations with the group during their next luncheon. "We, the white man, were the visitors and took everything from them, it's not right! Now our native people live on plots of land of no use to the white man to eke out a living."

Her further study documented the introduction of liquor, "fire water," that was initially provided by the Mexicans and white man. Now many Native Americans were alcoholics. They also have the highest incidence of diabetes of any population, whites, blacks, Asians, or Hispanics. Another gift the white man brought, she though frustration growing.

CHAPTER THIRTY

As Katie pondered the information fresh in her mind from her studies, her cell phone rang. It startled her; she didn't know she could get cell phone service at the campsite.

"Hello," she said, sort of in a huff because of the interruption, but when she realized it was Harold, she regained her composure.

"It's so nice to be able to get hold a hold of you."

"It's so nice, yet a surprise to hear your voice," she told Harold. It felt good to speak with someone fair-minded and she shared what she had uncovered to update him.

Harold listened patiently and told her how fascinated he was by her research. "Do you have the information documented somewhere? I'd like to study it. It might be helpful in my law practice when serving Native American people in court," he said.

They talked for a while and when they said goodbye, it saddened her slightly. "Harold has such a caring heart," she thought.

"I have found joy in life again, with time to grieve, eavesdrop on the trees and discover the unexpected; it allowed me to find my new self," she said out loud, as if conversing with nature. Katie pondered the fact that her home away from home, the membership RV site that once served as a retreat for her and Dan, now provided solace for her. It had given her family the ability to get away from their hectic schedules. "Now, it fascinates me to delve beyond the here and now. What seemed like a never ending hollowness has now given me the opportunity to discover a renewed self." She then whispered a silent prayer of thanksgiving.

Katie watched the covey of quail scurry across the road with their top knots bobbing up and down while they chatted in their soothing who-who language, something Casey always enjoyed. The squirrels also provided their entertainment. She watched the tree squirrels with their bushy gray tails, switching back and forth as they searched for food, and the way they scampered up the trees at any unfamiliar sound. The ground squirrels were different as they dug in the dirt and looked for buried hidden treasures. Nature offers a healing environment and she was thankful for the tender care it provided.

"Each time I return to Silent Glen it provides me with a totally new feeling and perspective. No longer do I feel the necessity to escape, but instead, I allow myself to ponder the pleasure that surrounds me and the joy it now provides." Katie continued to allow the tree groves to bathe her mind and allow her thoughts drift like an eagle soaring far above the earth.

CHAPTER THIRTY-ONE

Katie worked more from her home computer now instead of her laptop. She found less and less time to enjoy her motorhome but continued to contemplate her journey; periodically she heard the lullaby and flute with a feeling of a spiritual presence. The ethereal comfort bathed Katie with the feeling of freshness like one would feel after a spring rain.

Dan's belongings were gone except for a few of the special things that were kept in a box in the back of Katie's closet. She had completed the task a few months prior but hadn't been able to tackle her daughter's room. She told herself, "I'll start tomorrow," but tomorrow seemed to always slip away. The hollowness in her chest had lessened to a dull ache, where once it had engulfed her entire being each and every time she entered Casey's room. She had once sat on her daughter's bed and held the soft, stuffed rabbit, Casey's favorite, without turning into a blithering idiot. She would work on the computer for a while and promised herself to begin in Casey's room, "It will be my top priority early tomorrow morning."

Katie continued to be disheartened because of her inability to find information about those who had occupied the Silent Glen and Poppet Flats area. I can find documentation relating to the Soboba, San Manuel, and Morongo tribes, and part of the Cahuilla Nation, but not a thing on the Ivah natives. Maybe the people, if they did survive, were integrated into one or more of the other tribes. No concrete evidence could be found and she said it out loud as if trying to convince the computer to spit out some hidden facts.

At three in the morning when she looked up from her studies, her neck and back ached from her bent posture over the computer. She got ready for bed and took a couple of Motrin to loosen her tight muscles. She stretched like a cat who had bathed in the sun.

As she began to doze, the familiar serenity and peace embraced her. It's now time to completely release the dead and concentrate on the living, she thought as she drifted into the cloud of sleep. The resulting step would be to get completely through her daughter's room, her last thought as she floated into a dream state.

The next morning, as she reluctantly opened Casey's closet, she heard a knock at the door. There on her front porch stood Samantha with a wide grin and an older woman with graying hair at her temples.

"Come in" Katie, said and opened the door wider.

"Hi, I'm Lilly, Samantha's grandmother and I understand Sam's has visited you."

Katie pleased that they interrupted her task, offered coffee and cookies to Lilly and milk and cookies to Sam.

She enjoyed inviting people into her home and eventually she showed Sam her daughter's treasure chest.

"I've heard a lot about this treasure chest," Lilly said.

Later, as Katie entered the living room with the trunk, Sam shouted, "that's it!"

Sam approached it as if it was a momentous event, tenderly opened the chest and picked up the red dress. "This is my friends' favorite dress" Sam said. As Sam took out each article, Katie and Lilly talked and enjoyed watching Sam's delight in the contents of the box. Lilly told Katie she remained concerned that Sam was making a nuisance of herself, but Katie reassured her that not the case.

"Sam gives me a renewed purpose and provides a breath of fresh air as I make my way through changes. "It's taken time to resolve my sorrow and address a different life," she told Lily. Katie then continued to explain the journey she had traveled in the loss of her family. She said, "I will again have the pleasure of sharing the joy a little girl." Even a greater impact was the fact that Sam reported her continued visits by her angelic friend, the one who looked like her daughter. How else could Sam know the intimate details of the special times and things they shared? "It amazes me that children possess a unique receptive ability, without fear of the unknown. That innocent faith then enables others to enjoyment life even in the midst of resolving sorrow."

Lilly explained Sam spent most of her time with her because of her parents work schedule. Unfortunately, she and her husband would be moving to a smaller place, a residence for fifty-five and above. Sam's grandfather had suffered from a moderate stoke the year before and it left him weak on the left side. The home Lily and her husband shared had four bedrooms and half an acre of land, too much to keep because of his declining health.

Katie watched as Sam enjoyed Casey's treasures and asked Lilly if she would allow Sam to receive the chest as her gift. "Are you sure? That was your daughter's. Don't you want to keep them?"

"Absolutely not, they need to be loved and it is obvious Sam will enjoy and prize them", Katie told her with a radiate smile. "It lightens my heart to see Sam enjoy the things Casey once loved."

When the two left, Sam gave Katie a huge hug and said with sparkling eye," I'll take good care of these gifts and share them with all of her friends."

Katie invited them to come back any time, even after her grandparents moved.

Lilly thanked Katie, "you have been so generous. We definitely will keep in touch so Sam can visit."

During the conversation with Lilly, Katie suggested giving Sam some of her daughters' clothes.

"I'll need to check with Sam's mother for approval first, but I think she might appreciate it," Lily told Katie.

The chest of dress-up clothes would be treasured, just like it once had been, Katie thought. She repeated to Lily her desire to have Casey's clothing go to someone like Sam; someone who would appreciate and use them. Lilly would let her know. Katie suggested that when Sam's mother came to pick her up later that afternoon, Lilly introduce them so Katie could reassure Sam's mother and explain how pleased it would make Katie if Sam's mother agreed to the gift.

Katie allowed her mind to wander. "I can feel the deep healing of my soul and it continues to be evident to me as I take each baby step toward recovery. Time continues to heal the tremendous pain I once had as I let go of the past and venture into my unknown future. Now it doesn't frighten me as much. I will always miss Dan and Casey, but I no longer feel immobilized by the weight of losing them," she told herself, as she returned to Cassey's room to resume her task.

She took a deep breath as if to cleanse the remaining sorrow from her lungs and as she did, a smile lifted her lips and her heart felt lighter.

CHAPTER THIRTY-TWO

Katie dressed for her date, selecting a pair of tan slacks, a light cotton-candy-pink silk blouse with a matching sweater, and a pearl necklace in multicolor beige, pink, white and pale green with earrings to match. She pulled her hair back from her face with small pearl combs and the pastel colors of the outfit nicely enhanced the hazel of her eyes. "I can't remember when I last paid this much attention to my wardrobe and the way I look, and with such purpose," she thought.

When she arrived at the restaurant, her stomach felt tied in knots and perspiration collected at the nape of her neck, "I'm so nervous", she thought. "I need to gain my confidence, he's a nice man and it's only dinner."

She and Harold had each agreed to drive their own car and meet by the Koi pond in the front of the restaurant. As Katie approached, she noticed him standing just beyond the bridge watching the fish swim lazily in the water. He glanced up with a welcoming smile, then handed her a single pink rose.

They each let out a huge sigh of relief, and began to laugh. "I haven't dated in years," Harold said.

Katie told him, "I've been apprehensive as well." Their laughter broke the ice and the tension in her shoulders released as if a large load had been lifted. Harold took her elbow and guided her inside.

They were seated on the patio where a combo played soft jazz, some oldies-but-goodies and some big-band era music plus more modern music as well.

As she and Harold sipped their cocktails, they began to relax more and more. Katie ordered Ahi Tuna and Harold, Atlantic salmon.

"We will also have a bottle of your Alapay 2011 Lagrein from French Camp Vineyards in Paso Robles, if you please," Harold told the waiter. They chatted comfortably throughout dinner.

After they dined Harold took her hand and asked. "Would you like to dance?"

"That would be nice." She fit comfortably into his embrace. Katie sighed. "This is beautiful" she said, in almost a whisper. "The city lights below twinkle like multifaceted gems. The breeze is so soft and cool that it reminds me of the beach and the music is hypnotic." They enjoyed the evening dancing and talking until the band eventually completed their set.

They indulged in the chocolate lava cake for dessert and both seemed lost in their own thoughts.

When it became too cool to stay outside, they went inside and sat in a rich burgundy leather booth.

As the conversation continued, Katie asked Harold about his wife and he sighed with a faraway look in his eyes. "I feel guilty that I wasn't with her" he said. "Gloria went to visit her sister Ruth for two weeks in New York, but before she left she told me she might be pregnant. When she returned home we were going to get one of those urine tests to confirm it."

"Gloria was excited because she had never been out of California before, and Ruth was also thrilled, she would be able to show her little sister the 'Big Apple.' They planned to see a Broadway show, Times Square, The Statue of Liberty, Ellis Island, and ride the train to Grand Central Station, visit the Empire State Building as well as the United Nations with all of their flags. Gloria wanted to see it all. I was tied up with an ongoing Medicare fraud case that had lasted over a year so I couldn't go with her."

"I was in court when the first plane hit the tower. After the news hit the TV, court immediately adjourned and we went to the judge's chamber. There everyone watched the TV in horror as the second plane struck the other tower and that unforgettable day unfolded. I tried to reach her sister Ruth, but the phone lines were down and Gloria's cell phone didn't pick up either. Chaos reigned as the debris rained down from the buildings. Because I couldn't reach either Gloria or her sister I tried one of my associates but remembered his office was on the twenty-second floor of the first tower. It no longer existed."

"There was nothing I could do but wait. With all planes grounded I couldn't get to New York. I continued to be persistent, attempting to contact my wife or sister-in-law, but wasn't successful. My frustration grew to a feverish peak, as did that of all who had loved ones in New York.

"Gloria was to arrive at the Ontario Airport in two days but no planes flew for five or six days. When her plane eventually arrived, she was not on it, and then I knew."

Katie watched as tears filled Harold's eyes and slid aimlessly down his cheeks. He continued. "Their deaths weren't confirmed, but when Ruth's landlord called me to report she'd never returned to her apartment, it became a fact."

Harold told Katie he caught the first available plane east and spent the next month in search of information. "A friend of Ruth's, Andrea, said she had intended to be with Ruth and Gloria to tour the towers, but she had caught the flu, and couldn't make it. She was too sick."

Harold continued the horrible story. "Because Gloria and Ruth's elderly parents were dead, it was just the two sisters: it then became my responsibility to clear out Ruth's apartment. Ruth's friends helped. I left everything there except the family jewelry and a few mementos. The apartment owner was grateful for a furnished flat to rent and her friends distributed her personal items and clothing. Andrea promised to send the antique radio and dental cabinet and any other family valuables to me as they continued to go through Ruth's apartment."

Harold now cried openly. "It was the hardest thing I ever had to do, especially when facing the task of going through her things when I returned home."

Katie patted Harold's hand as tears slid down her cheeks. She remembered all too well the pain she experienced as she went through Daniel and Casey's belongings. They shared so much in common.

Harold asked her to share the story of her family's death. He knew they died in a car accident but didn't know the specifics. It was now her turn to unburden her heart. She felt comfortable now that he would understand. Harold nodded knowingly as she shared her tragic story.

They enjoyed each other's pictures of their loved ones, sharing funny things that happened and discussing the journey of grief and what each had endured. They laughed a lot and discovered they both suffered from survivor's guilt for having put work before family.

Harold looked pointedly at Katie with a surprised expression at what he was about to say. "Work is just part of who we are and a fact of life. We all strive to achieve and it shouldn't make us feel guilty about where we were, we could have been at home or at the store or even in the shower. What we need to hold onto is the love that we shared." Katie agreed and it was obvious a great burden had been lifted from each of them by the way each took a deep breath and sat a little taller in the booth.

After dinner, dessert and their long soul-baring conversation, Harold walked Katie to her car and gave her a bear hug. "I'd like to see you again!" he said.

She responded as a shy smile crossed her lips and grew broader and her eyes twinkled in the moonlight. "I would love to, when?"

Every time they were together their comfort and enjoyment grew and each appreciated just being alive. "It feels good to share my deepest feeling with you while enjoying your companionship," she told Harold. He seconded her statement then she got into the car then drove away, as he waved goodbye. "Life is good" she told herself, contented.

CHAPTER THIRTY-THREE

Katie's trip to Silent Glen hadn't been planned. She sat on the large table-like rock the Indians had once used to prepare food. The wind whistled through the trees and the air felt like satin as it flowed over her skin. The sounds in the trees reminded her of the ancestry of the mountain and those who preceded her, as well as the tale they now shared.

"Fascinating, that life goes on after tragedy and now, maybe the reason I have experienced the visions and mountain lore is to help me with my own life. What a gift I have received." Katie thought.

"My family will always be part of me and forever make up who I am. Daniel would want me to live, not just exist."

"I'm now sure Harold and I have been brought together to heal. Maybe we will just be friends, but as time passes it seems likely it will become more. Perhaps there will be a fresh beginning, a new life, when I can again share myself and create a fresh start."

Katie pondered all the revealing thoughts and transformed feelings, as she observed the leaves in the exquisite oak trees. They moved and swayed as if in concert with one another, whispering from tree to tree as the light breeze conducted their tale. "Yes, I have been privileged to discover myself through the tale of the trees."

About the Author
Cathie Norton

Cathie Norton is a retired registered nurse, having had a creative 45 years profession that began in the intensive care unit, cardiac rehab, and emergency room. She served as a liaison, tele-health coordinator, educator and case manager and eventually retiring from hospice. To this day, she still volunteers in a local hospital.

Cathie enjoys singing in her church choir, working with stained glass beads, and cooking.

She is happily married to her best friend of 47 years, Newell, who has been her greatest advocate and encouraged her to embark on a writing career. They have two terrific sons, Bryan and Brett, and six amazing grandchildren. Cathie is a native Californian.

Learn more about Cathie at her website:

www.CathieNorton.com